Whatever After

ONCE UPON A FROG

Read all the *Whatever After* books!

#1: Fairest of All

#2: If the Shoe Fits

#3: Sink or Swim

#4: Dream On

#5: Bad Hair Day

#6: Cold as Ice

#7: Beauty Queen

#8: Once Upon a Frog

#9: Genie in a Bottle

Whatever After

ONCE UPON A FROG

SARAH MLYNOWSKI

Scholastic Inc.

ISBN 978-1-338-03596-4

10 9 8 7 6 5 4 3 2 1   16 17 18 19 20

Printed in the U.S.A.   40
First printing 2016

for the downtown bus kids!

priya dattilio, sofie dewan, margot eilian,
alex goldsmith, natalie hecker,
aidan rosenblatt, jared rosenblatt,
bennett roy, henry saadi sheppard
(and chloe swidler)

we read and sing songs
and think mad libs are fun.
we bounce in our seats,
and we love to chew gum.

xoxo

* chapter one *

Crabby Abby

"Oh, Crabby Abby . . ."

Ugh. I hate when he calls me that.

I look up from the book of Mad Libs on my lap to see Brandon Walters walking across the school yard toward me. Two minutes ago, I saw him spinning Luke Silver superfast on one of the tire swings. Luke was shouting, "Stop!" but Brandon kept spinning him faster and faster until Luke looked like he might throw up.

Did the recess monitor see this? No. Her view of the tire swings was blocked by a big group of kids playing four square.

So not only did Brandon not get in trouble, but now he's right here. I look back down and pretend I don't see his red hair and freckled face in front of me.

"What are you doing, Crabby Abby?"

My shoulders tense. What I'm doing is sitting on a bench with my friends, minding my own business. I glance back up. Even though it's winter, it's so sunny that I have to squint. Brandon fake-squints back at me. Who knows what he'll say or do?

This morning in class, I dropped my eraser, and Brandon kicked it across the room. Then he stuck his tongue out at me. All when our teacher wasn't looking, of course.

I glance at Frankie on my left and at Robin on my right. Both my best friends look equally worried. "We're doing Mad Libs, Brandon."

Do I want to spend the last five minutes of recess listening to Brandon call me Crabby Abby? No, I do not. Frankie, Robin, and I have been working on this page for ten minutes, and there are only a few spaces left.

I decide to try and ignore him, and I stare at the blank space on the page. *The ____________ (adjective) girl is sitting at the table eating a ____________ (food) sandwich.* "Who has an adjective?" I ask. "That's a word that describes a noun."

"I've got one," Brandon says, looking at Robin. "Stupid! That's S-T-U-P-I-D, for kids who aren't that great at spelling."

Robin blushes, and I give Brandon a dirty look. That was a shot at Robin, because she has to go to a writing tutor. But Robin is not stupid at all. She's really smart. She's one of the best scientists in our class.

"And another one," Brandon adds, looking right at Frankie. "Four-eyed." He cups his hands around his eyes, obviously making fun of Frankie's glasses (which are totally cute, by the way). Then he laughs and slaps his knee. "I'm hilarious! Hey, that's another adjective."

"Is 'annoying' an adjective?" Robin snaps.

"How about 'mean'?" Frankie suggests, fixing the barrette in her dark hair.

"Both work," I say, narrowing my eyes at Brandon.

Brandon sticks out his tongue at all of us. "Let me see those Mad Libs," he orders.

"No," I say. "We're in the middle of it."

Instead of listening, Brandon reaches over and grabs the book from my hand.

"Hey!" I yell, jumping up. "Give it back!"

He smirks and holds the book above his head, which is way above mine.

When he finally lowers it, he says, "Ah . . . ah . . . ah . . . CHOO!" And sneezes all over my Mad Libs book.

"Gross!" Robin cries.

"So gross," Frankie adds, wrinkling up her face.

Gross is definitely an adjective.

Brandon laughs. "You can have it back now, Crabby Abby," he says, handing it to me.

UGGGGGGH. "Thanks but no thanks," I grumble. Do I want his nasty germs all over my Mad Libs? No, I do not. I toss the book in the garbage. There was still one whole Mad Lib left, too.

"Do you want me to finish it for you?" Brandon asks. "How about, a *smelly* girl is sitting at a table eating a *snot* sandwich!" He laughs again. No one else finds it funny. Because it's NOT. Thankfully, he turns around then and leaves, probably to go torment someone else.

"He's such a jerk," Robin mutters.

"He really is," I say. He wasn't always. At least, he was never this bad. But in the last few weeks, he's called all the kids names, knocked over peoples' food at lunch, and thrown balls over the fence at gym and recess.

Have we done anything to deserve it? No, we have not!

I am trying to take the high road and just ignore him. But sometimes I wish I had magic powers and could cast a spell on him.

Okay, I know that sounds unlikely. But I've seen people do it.

Really.

See, I have a magic mirror in my basement. And when my little brother and I sneak downstairs at midnight and knock on the mirror three times, the mirror hisses, turns purple, and swirls. Then it sucks me and my little brother into fairy tales.

Also our dog, Prince.

Every time we go, Maryrose takes us into a different fairy tale. Maryose is the fairy who lives inside our mirror. At least we think she lives inside our mirror. We're not totally clear about her housing situation. Anyway, so far, she's taken us into the stories of *Snow White*, *Cinderella*, *The Little Mermaid*, *Sleeping Beauty*, *Rapunzel*, *The Snow Queen*, and *Beauty and the Beast*. And in many of the fairy tales, there is someone, a fairy usually, who has magical powers and can turn people into all kinds of stuff.

Like a beast. Yup. I've seen it. I've BEEN it. Seriously — I've actually been turned into a beast. I had fur, I had claws, I had it all.

So when Brandon does something especially jerky, I imagine turning him into a beast. Or a rat. Or maybe an ant that I could step on.

I shake off that thought. No, I wouldn't step on him. But I might put him in a box with air holes and some grass or whatever ants eat and forget about him for a while.

The bell rings, and Frankie, Robin, and I line up. Ahead, I can hear Penny, Robin's other best friend, shouting, "Stop it, Brandon!"

I lean out to see what he's doing. Brandon is stepping on the backs of Penny's shoes. One of her sneakers is half off her foot. Do I like that Robin has another best friend? No. Do I even LIKE Penny? No again. But should Brandon be bothering Penny? No, no, NO.

"You're such a pain!" Penny yells, moving her blond ponytail to the side. Brandon probably yanked it. She steps out of line and joins me, Frankie, and Robin near the end. "I've told on him twice," she says, "and the teachers never do anything!"

It's true. We might have to take matters into our own hands.

Maybe the next time I go through the mirror, I'll bring home a magic wand.

* chapter two *

Itchy Memories

I'm still irritated at the end of the day when my brother, Jonah, and I are standing outside school, waiting for our dad to pick us up.

It doesn't help when Brandon says, "Bye, Crabby Abby," as he strolls past me. He walks home from school by himself. Either his parents trust him to make his way home alone or they think he's awful, too, and are hoping he gets kidnapped.

"Crabby Abby!" Jonah repeats, laughing. Jonah is seven. Of course he finds that funny.

"Don't call me Crabby Abby," I mutter.

"But you *can* be crabby."

"Don't call me that!" I repeat. Though I guess I *can* be crabby. But who doesn't get crabby sometimes? Jonah definitely does.

"Okay, okay," Jonah says. "But why was he teasing you?"

I watch as Brandon, his neon-yellow backpack over one shoulder, turns the corner. He's finally out of sight. "Because he's horrible," I reply. "He sneezed all over my Mad Libs! On purpose! It was disgusting."

Jonah gets the strange look on his face. It's a look I'm getting used to. Like he's watching a movie inside his head.

"Are you remembering something?" I ask.

Jonah nods.

When we were on our way home from *Beauty and the Beast*, Jonah was reverse hypnotized by the swirling mirror and got some of Maryrose's memories. Yup. My brother has a fairy's memories. In his brain. But he doesn't remember everything all the time. He only remembers some stuff, when something he sees triggers a memory.

"When you said *sneezed on your Mad Libs*, I remembered something!" Jonah exclaims.

"What?" I ask excitedly. Who knew grimy snot germs on my Mad Libs could be a good thing?

"When Maryrose was little, Jax sneezed in her *face*!" Jonah says.

Jax is also a fairy, and he's Maryrose's cousin. He's not very nice. Jonah and I met him in *Beauty and the Beast*.

Jonah scratches his head. Ever since the memories started coming, Jonah's had a head itch. The itching gets worse when the memories pop up.

"And then," Jonah goes on, his eyes wide, still scratching his head, "Maryrose got sick and had to spend two weeks in bed! Her bed was really cool. It floated just below the ceiling! She had to take a ladder up to it, and she had to use a slide to get down."

"Just great," I say with a sigh. "Another terrifically unhelpful memory."

You'd think Jonah having some of Maryrose's memories would be useful. Like maybe he could remember why Maryrose lives in our mirror. Or how Maryrose brings us into different fairy tales. Or *why* Maryrose brings us into different fairy tales.

But no. Instead, Jonah remembers useless information. Like how Maryose's cousin got her sick. And what her bed looked like.

Last week, a rip in Jonah's sweatshirt reminded him that Maryrose once ripped her scarf on a twig.

And eating a blueberry yogurt made him remember that Maryrose once had blueberry pie.

Those memories were of no help to us.

"Was this your first memory of the day?" I ask.

Jonah shakes his head, frowning. "I got one during math. I was counting on my fingers, and I remembered that Maryrose likes to ride a bike with no hands!"

"Huh? Why did you remember that?

"I guess my fingers made me remember her hands. I don't know! It's not an exact science. But then Mr. Gordon called on me to answer a question about subtracting two digit numbers, and I realized I hadn't heard a word he'd said. I had to write him a note promising I would pay attention in class. Don't tell Mom or Dad."

Poor Jonah. This has been happening a lot these past two weeks. He even had an office detention because of "not listening." All because he has someone else's memories in his head. My parents had a big talk with him about paying attention and canceled a playdate as punishment. But it's not his fault.

"This is starting to not be that fun," Jonah says. He scratches the back of his head again.

We haven't been down to the mirror in two weeks. I've been avoiding Maryrose. I'm nervous that she won't like the fact that Jonah has her memories. I mean, come on. I would hate it if someone had my memories! It's creepy!

What if Maryrose decides she doesn't want some kid running around with all of her memories? Sure, she seems nice so far, but how do we know she really *is* nice? We don't!

Not all fairies are nice. That we *do* know.

But maybe I'm wrong. Maybe it's a test. Maybe Maryrose is waiting to see if we'll come to her and tell her the truth.

And Jonah does seem to be suffering . . .

"Let's try to talk to Maryrose tonight," I say, coming to a decision. "We'll knock on the mirror to let her know we need to talk to her. But we won't go *through* the mirror."

We promised our parents we wouldn't get out of bed in the middle of the night and "play" in the basement. And we keep our promises. At least we try to.

But we *have* to talk to Maryrose. Enough is enough! Jonah can't fail second grade and get in trouble all the time because he has a fairy's memories.

"Sounds good to me," Jonah says. "You sure you don't want to go through the mirror?"

Our dad pulls up and I wave to him. Then I nod at Jonah. "Yeah. We have to do our best to keep our promise. Just talking. No trips into fairy tales this time. For sure."

* chapter three *

Wait for Me!

At eleven fifty-nine P.M., Jonah and I are standing in our basement in front of the magic mirror. Both of us are breathing hard and our dog, Prince, is panting.

We almost slept through the midnight deadline. I thought I'd set my alarm clock for ten minutes ago, but either I forgot to, or it's broken. Luckily, Prince woke me up by jumping on my bed and licking my foot. Good dog!

Prince is *such* a good dog that he was super quiet as we raced down the stairs, then through the door to the basement and down another flight of steps. Our parents stayed fast asleep. They may have caught us in the basement at a crazy hour once, but they still don't know about the magic mirror. Well, they knew about it for about five seconds once, but then Maryrose hypnotized them and they forgot all about it.

The mirror is about twice the size of me and attached to the wall with heavy bolts. It has a stone frame that's engraved with small fairies with wings and wands. In the smooth glass part, I can see our reflections. I'm wearing flannel pj bottoms and a long-sleeved gray sleep shirt. Jonah is wearing his Superman pajamas. We are both barefoot.

I'd thought *Jonah*'s hair was a mussed-up mess as I got him out of bed. But in the mirror, I can see that my curly brown hair is even crazier-looking than his.

"Should we knock?" Jonah asks. "Is it time?"

"Yes!" I say, but then I sneak a peek at my watch to make sure.

Oops.

I'm not wearing my watch.

I knock once. "Maryrose? Are you there?" I call.

Hissssss, the mirror says.

Oh, good! A response. Kind of.

"Hi, Maryrose!" I say. "It's us. Jonah and Abby. And, um,

Prince." Our dog barks. "We wanted to tell you something. Are you there?"

Another *hissssssssss*.

"She's hissing," Jonah says. "But she's not talking. You know, she usually only talks to us when we get *back* from the fairy tale. Not before."

"Maybe we should knock once more," I say. I knock a second time. A purple glow spreads over the room. "Maryrose? Are you there? Can we talk? We have something important to tell you about your memories!"

She doesn't answer.

"Should we knock a third time?" Jonah asks.

"If we knock a third time, the mirror will start to pull us inside," I point out, getting worried.

"So?"

"So . . ." I hesitate. "Do we *want* to go into a fairy tale? Even though we promised Mom and Dad we wouldn't?"

Jonah scratches his head. "If that's how to get Maryrose to talk to us, then yes. I can't go on like this! I just had *another* memory, about Maryrose trying on a coat in front of a mirror. I'm so itchy!" He scratches again, his hair sticking up even more.

"Well . . . technically, we promised Mom and Dad we wouldn't go into the basement at night. And we've already broken that promise."

"Many times," Jonah says.

"Okay," I say. "Let's do it. Let me just get my watch from upstairs first."

We can't go into the fairy tales without a watch. Fairy tale time is different from real life time. Sometimes a day in a fairy tale is an hour at home. Sometimes it's half a day at home. A watch keeps track of the time in Smithville. I had to trade my last watch for cab fare a few fairy tales ago. But I saved up for a new one with my allowance.

"Stay here. I'll be right back," I say, and Jonah nods. Prince wags his tail.

I bolt up the stairs. As long as Jonah doesn't knock a third time, the mirror should keep swirling for a little bit longer. I figure I have thirty seconds.

I dash into my room and race to my jewelry box. It's decorated with drawings of fairy tale characters. Like Cinderella. Rapunzel. Snow White. Except Snow White is wearing my old lime-green pajamas. See, Jonah and I somehow always mess up the stories we enter. Luckily, by the time we get home, we manage to help the characters find new happy endings.

Somehow, the characters on my jewelry box always change to show what happens after Jonah and I return home.

I open the lid, but the watch isn't in the jewelry box. Crumbs! It's not on my desk. Or on my dresser. Where is it? My room isn't that messy. Where are you, watch? I stand in the center of the room, looking around everywhere.

Oh! Shoes! I see shoes! I'm not wearing any shoes and I should be! I shove my feet into my flip-flops while I look around for the watch. Oh! I left it on my nightstand!

That's when I hear my brother shout, "Abby!!!!!"

I hold my breath, expecting our parents to come rushing out of their bedroom to see what's wrong. But no doors open. No footsteps. Phew.

I'm coming, Jonah! I yell in my head since I don't want to scream it out loud and wake my parents.

I grab my new watch off the nightstand. Buckling the orange-and-white strap onto my wrist, I spin around and run down one flight, turn, then race through the basement door and down the second, and —

Jonah and Prince are gone.

And the mirror is swirling furiously like it does after three knocks.

AHHHHH!

What happened? Why did they go without me? Jonah never goes without me!

What if I land in a different fairy tale? What do I do then?

"Maryrose! Are you there?" I whisper-yell at the swirling purple haze in the mirror.

Silence.

"Maryrose! I need you!" I whisper-yell again. But she doesn't appear in the mirror. "Will I land in the same fairy tale that Jonah and Prince are in?"

No answer.

The mirror is still swirling. It's pulling me toward it as if it's a vacuum cleaner and I'm a piece of carpet fluff.

I have to find Jonah and Prince! I have to!

Without further hesitation, I jump in.

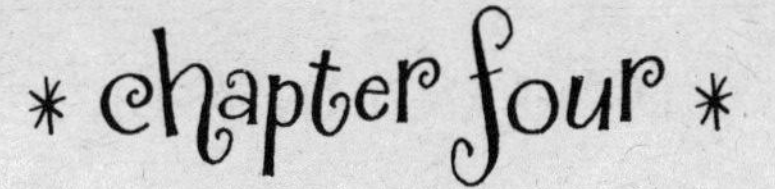

Well, Hello

I land with a hard splash.

Ouch.

Water soaks through the bottom of my pj's. Argh. At least my watch is waterproof.

I quickly stand up and try to look around for Jonah and Prince. But it's dark in here. And definitely wet. The water goes up to my knees.

"Jonah? Prince? Hello?" I yell out. My voice echoes.

Silence.

Oh no. Oh no. Oh no.

WHAT IF I DID LAND IN A DIFFERENT FAIRY TALE?

Maybe Maryrose was mad at Jonah for having her memories and wanted to punish him? What if she's mad at me for not telling her about Jonah's memories sooner and wanted to punish me? What if I never see my brother again? What will I tell my *parents*?

Agh!

"Jonah?" I call out.

No answer.

My legs start shaking. My wet legs. My pajama bottoms are stuck to me and the water squishes through my flip-flops.

Ewww — what is that slimy thing on my big toe? I kick, and a green frog leaps onto a leaf.

I shiver. I'm in some kind of tiny, dark lake with a frog. Maybe there are snakes, too. I hate snakes! Does anyone like snakes?

"Jonah!" I yell out again. My heart is pounding. Where is my brother?

Okay, calm down, Abby, I order myself. *Figure out where you are.*

I press my hands up against a nearby wall. It feels like stone. The room itself is small. Only a few feet wide. And it's circular.

Am I in a tiny, watery dungeon?

I glance up. Probably not — no bars at the top. And there's blue sky above me.

Am I in a tunnel? No. Tunnels run sideways, not up and down.

Am I in a . . . well?

Yes! I look back down at the water. I think I *am* in a well. Okay, at least I know where I am. Not that it helps.

"Jonah!" I yell again. "Prince!"

I listen for Prince's *ruff*, but I hear nothing.

I stare up at the rim of the well, hoping I'll suddenly see Jonah's face. But I don't.

If my palms weren't damp from well water, they'd be damp from fear.

I hate being separated from my brother.

Wait a minute. We went in through the same swirl, even if it wasn't at the same time, so maybe that means we ARE in the same fairy tale. Maybe Jonah and Prince did land someplace nearby but I can't see them because I'm stuck in this tiny well.

Uh-oh.

They couldn't be underwater, could they? I crouch back down. The water isn't deep enough to get lost in. It's only to my knees. I would see a little kid and a furry dog if they were below the surface.

I kick my feet around just to make sure. No Jonah and no Prince.

I stand back up. "JONAH!" I yell as loud as I can.

"Abby?" I hear Jonah say. "Where are you?"

Yes! I feel a burst of relief. He's here! We *are* in the same fairy tale! But where *is* he exactly?

"Jonah! I'm down here!" I shout, standing on my toes and waving my arms.

"Huh? I can hear you, but I can't see you!" Jonah calls back.

"I'm in the well!"

My neck is strained from leaning my head back and staring up at the top of the well, but finally, Jonah's face appears over the rim. Yay! I've never been so happy to see my little brother's face!

"Hi!" I say, waving up at him. A fly buzzes in my ear, and I swat it away.

"Hi!" Jonah calls down, grinning. "There you are! I was worried you wouldn't come through the mirror!"

Suddenly, I hear a familiar *Ruff, ruff, ruff!* Prince appears over the edge of the well, too, his tongue hanging out of his mouth.

"Hi, sweetie!" I call up. "I'm so glad you're both okay!" Then my relief turns to annoyance. "Why'd you guys go through the mirror without me? You're not allowed to go without me!"

"Sorry!" Jonah says. He reaches over and pats Prince's head. "This little guy wagged his tail into the mirror, and I guess that counted as the third knock. The mirror started to swirl superfast and then we got sucked in!"

"*Mrowwwwww*," Prince says, with big puppy dog eyes.

Aw, I can't stay mad at him. "Okay, you're both forgiven. But don't let it happen again."

"How'd you get down there, anyway?" Jonah asks.

That's the thing with getting sucked into fairy tales. We never know exactly where we'll end up. We don't know which fairy tale we'll fall into or *where* in the fairy tale we'll fall. "No idea," I call up. "How'd you get up *there*?"

"No clue," he says. "We landed near a tree."

Seeing Jonah above helps orient me. The well feels about three times my height. I'm four and a half feet tall. Which means the well is about thirteen and a half feet deep.

Too bad my math skills aren't going to help me get out of this well. "Can you look around for something you can use to help me out of here?" I ask Jonah.

"'Kay! Be right back!"

Ruff? my dog says, tilting his head at me.

"Go with him, Prince!" I say. "He needs your help."

Prince bounds away.

"Who needs my help?" an unfamiliar voice asks.

An unfamiliar voice right next to me.

But the only thing next to me is the frog I saw before. The frog is perched on a leaf. Staring at me with its big, bulgy, amber-brown eyes.

The voice I heard must have been Jonah playing a trick on me. I look up at the top of the well. But I don't see my brother anymore. But how did Jonah make his voice go that deep and croaky and come from so close?

"Very funny, Jonah," I call up. "No more jokes! Just keep an eye on Prince, okay?"

"I am the prince!" the unfamiliar voice says.

AGAIN FROM RIGHT NEXT TO ME.

I jump back, flattening myself against the wall of the well.

The frog is staring at me. And I think he's smiling. Do frogs smile?

I stare back.

A frog just talked to me! At least, I think it did. Unless I hit my head on my way in. "Did you say something?" I ask the frog.

"Yes," he says puffing up his chest. "You mentioned a prince, and I'm a prince. I know it's difficult to imagine in my current condition, but it's the truth."

I can clearly see him moving his froggy lips. The frog is definitely talking.

He's about the size of a fist, green with a few brown spots on his back. Big for a frog. Not that I've seen that many frogs up close. He's really kind of . . . cute. Elegant, really. He's squatting, his four little legs on the leaf, as if he might hop away at any moment.

"Y-y-you're a prince?" I stammer.

He tilts his head and stares back at me. "Yes," he responds. "Hello."

I'm in a well. With a talking frog. A frog who claims to be a prince.

This can only mean one thing.

Not true. It could probably mean lots of things. Like I really did hit my head and am now hallucinating. Or that someone has planted a microphone inside a frog and is pretending to make him speak. But in this case, I'm willing to bet that it means . . .

We're in the story of *The Frog Prince*!

✻ chapter five ✻

The Real Story. Maybe.

Hurrah! I love that fairy tale! True, I love most fairy tales. But *The Frog Prince* is one of my favorites. There's a Disney movie based on it, too, but that's called *The Princess and the Frog.* The movie is totally different from the fairy tale. It's set in New Orleans and is about a regular girl named Tiana who turns into a frog after she kisses the frog prince.

But the original fairy tale, which my nana told me, starts with a princess. She is wandering around and drops her ball in a well. But there's a frog inside the well! The frog offers to get the ball for the princess if she'll be his friend and companion. She agrees. He gives her back the ball. But then she refuses to be his friend because he's a frog. The frog finds her at her castle and reminds her of her promise. The princess's father makes her keep the promise, so the princess takes the frog to her room, but she's annoyed. So annoyed that she throws the frog against the wall, and presto — he turns into a handsome prince.

Yup. That's the real story. People always think that the princess kisses the frog and *that's* what turns him back into a prince. But that's not what happens in the original story written by the Brothers Grimm. I don't know where the kissing part came from. There are lots of other versions of *The Frog Prince.* Maybe it was in one of those.

"Hello there!" I say to the frog, feeling excited. "It's so nice to meet you!"

"It's nice to meet you, too," he says. He bats his long eyelashes at me shyly. "I've been hoping someone would come along. Someone I can trust, that is. I can't talk to just anyone. I once tried to tell a boy my story and he lunged for me, saying he could probably sell a talking frog for a fortune."

"That's terrible!" I say. "Well, you can trust me," I assure him.

"You're probably wondering how a frog can talk," he says,

stretching out on the leaf. "I can talk because I'm actually human — well, I'm a human trapped inside the body of a frog."

Of course I know that part, but I'm fascinated to hear the rest. The original story was sketchy on the details.

The frog lifts his pointy green chin. "My name is Prince Frederic. I'm heir to the throne of my kingdom. At least I was, until an evil fairy turned me into a frog."

"But why?" I ask.

He hangs his head and looks like he might cry. "My own sister, Sophie, who wants the throne for herself, paid the evil fairy to do this to me."

"How awful!" I say. I think of how Mr. Beast from *Beauty and the Beast* was turned into a beast. "Why did the fairy turn you into a *frog*, though?" I ask.

"My kingdom is called Frogville. I suppose my sister has a bad sense of humor." Frederic laughs sadly. "Not long ago, I was sitting down to gourmet meals of steak and soufflés. Now I have to catch and eat flies." He flicks out his tongue and catches one with a snapping curl. "Don't think I find flies tasty just because I'm a frog. I definitely do *not*."

"I wouldn't think you did," I say, feeling very sorry for Prince

Frederic. He really is quite regal-looking, even as a frog. Yet here he is, hanging out in wells and munching on insects.

Frederic nods. Actual tears fill his big eyes. I never thought frogs could cry. Then again, I'd never imagined they could speak to people, either.

"All I want is to become human again," Frederic says. "To become a prince again. To return to my kingdom and save my dear people from my terrible sister. She doesn't care about anyone. She only values money and power. She is a tyrant. She locks everyone in prison! Even ten-year-old children!"

Oh, gosh. *I'm* ten. I would *not* want to go to prison.

Poor fly-eating Frederic! Poor ten-year-old children!

"I'm so sorry," I say. "That's terrible."

He perks up, his little froggy shoulders lifting. "Will you help turn me back into a human?" he asks hopefully.

"Me? No!"

His little froggy shoulders fall. "Oh."

I'd give him a big hug if I weren't afraid of crushing him. "Not because I don't want to! I know who will turn you back into a human and she's coming! Any minute! Really! She's going to drop her ball in the well. You'll catch it. When she asks you to give it back, tell her you'll give it to her only if she'll be your companion. Got it? Then you'll eventually get changed back into a person."

"Got it!" he says, nodding happily. "I would make an excellent companion. I'm extremely strong for a frog. I do a lot of push-ups. Want to see?"

"Sure . . ."

"Abby?" I hear from above.

I look up. My brother is peeking into the well again.

"Jonah! You're back! Do you have something to help get me out of here?"

"I couldn't find anything," he says. "I'll keep looking. I just wanted to check on you."

"I'm fine! Is Prince with you?"

"Yup," Jonah says. "He's chasing a bird. Oh! I think I figured out what story we're in. The trees are really tall here! Really, really tall. Tall enough for giants! I think we're finally in *Jack and the Beanstalk*!"

I snort. "We're not. I promise, we're not."

Jonah pouts. "How do you know?"

"Because I'm in a well. And I've been chatting with a talking frog. A talking, royal frog."

"So?"

Maybe Jonah hit *his* head on the way in.

"So . . . we're in *The Frog Prince*!"

"Oh," my brother says. "Boo. But, hello, talking frog!" He waves down into the well, his voice echoing.

"Hello, young man," the frog calls up. "I am Frederic."

"Hello, Frederic! I am Jonah!"

"And I am Abby," I say formally.

"And neither of you will be my companion?" Frederic asks. He seems a little sad again. Now I feel bad that *we* can't be the ones to turn him back into a prince.

"I will!" Jonah exclaims.

"No, you won't," I tell my brother with a sigh. "The *princess* is going to be his companion."

"Oh, right, Princess Tiana."

I shake my head. "No, not Princess Tiana. She's only in the movie version."

"Gotcha," Jonah says. "So another princess is going to come by? And then what? She kisses the frog?"

"No one's kissing anyone," I tell him. "But yes, another princess is about to come by. She'll be playing with a golden ball. She'll drop it in the well by accident. The frog will catch it. The story will go on the way it's supposed to. That's the way this works."

Jonah laughs. "Seriously? That's never the way this works! We always mess up the story."

That's true. We do. "But not on purpose!" I say.

"Sometimes on purpose," Jonah says.

I'm getting impatient. "Jonah, can we finish this debate once you've gotten me out of the well?"

"Okay," he says.

"Thank you!"

I'll definitely mess up the story if the princess sees me down here. When she drops the ball and it's thrown back up to her, she might think I did it. It's not like frogs are known for their throwing skills.

"Wait a minute," Frederic says to me. "Are you saying that Princess Cassandra is going to be my companion and turn me human?"

"Well, I don't know her name —" I begin.

"I've been trying to get her attention for days!" Frederic says. "Short blond hair? I thought I could talk to her, royal to royal. I thought maybe if I became her friend, she would help me. Maybe she'd force one of the fairies in her kingdom to turn me back. Or at least lend me the money to hire one of them. But she's such a fast rider on her horse that I can't keep up with her. I followed her here from her palace. And then I jumped down the well. I was hoping she'd get thirsty and stop to drink some well water and I'd finally be able to talk to her. That's why I came to this kingdom in the first place."

"How did you get here?" I ask him, curious.

"What do you mean?" he asks. "I hopped!"

I can't help but smile. "Well, your plan was smart," I tell him. "This well is exactly where you should be when the princess comes by. But it's exactly where I *shouldn't* be." I glance up at Jonah, who is still hovering over the well. "We have to get me out!"

"But how?" Jonah asks.

Good question. "I don't know. Don't wells normally have a bucket or something? Isn't that the point of wells? To bring stuff up in a bucket?" I ask.

"What stuff?" Jonah asks.

"Stuff!" I kick my heel and hear a splash. "Like water!"

"Hmm. That sounds right," Jonah says. "But I see no bucket."

Crumbs. "There's not one down here, either. What else is around you?"

I see Jonah's head turning left, then right. "It looks like a forest," he says. "But with really big trees. *Really* big ones. Giant ones. They could even be beanstalks! Are you sure we're not in *Jack and the* —"

"Jonah, we are NOT in *Jack and the Beanstalk*! I am stuck in a well with a TALKING FROG!"

"Fine," Jonah huffs. "It's really hot up here," he adds. "You might want to stay down there, know-it-all. Bet it's cooler."

My flannel pj bottoms are sticking to me. Not exactly comfortable. "I think I'd rather get out of the bottom of the well, thanks. Is there a rope out there?"

"No rope," he says. "Not much of anything."

I turn to Frederic. "Any ideas?"

"Can you climb up?" the frog suggests.

I feel the inside of the well to see if there are ridges or anything to dig my feet into, but it feels smooth. "Let me try," I say, and attempt to pull myself up. I can't. "I guess you wouldn't be able to give me a boost," I say to Frederic.

"My push-ups *have* made me strong," he reminds me. "But not that strong."

Ruff! Ruff, ruff! Ruff! I hear from above. *Ruff! Ruff, ruff! Ruff!*

Prince is barking the way he does when the doorbell rings. "What's wrong?" I call up to Jonah.

"Someone's coming!" Jonah says.

"It's probably the princess!" I cry. Crumbs. I was hoping to get out of here first. Now what? I have to hide. So do Prince and Jonah! "Go hide!" I tell my brother.

"Where?"

"You said you're in a forest. Go find a tree! Quick, so she doesn't see you!" I say. "We want the story to continue the way it's supposed to!"

Although what Jonah said before was right. We always mess up the stories.

"Whatever you say, Abby!" Jonah calls back. He ducks out of sight.

"Is she coming now?" Frederic asks. His bulging eyes look up, then back at me.

I nod. I listen for footsteps or voices but don't hear anything. The princess *has* to stop at the well. I take a deep breath. She will. It's part of the original story.

"Should *we* hide?" Frederic asks.

"Yes! No! I should hide. You should not. You have to do what I told you to."

"So I shouldn't just talk to her, royal to royal? Ask for her help?" Frederic asks.

"Well, you could," I say. "But you *are* a frog. What if she doesn't believe your story? Let's try it my way. Just remember: You're supposed to catch the ball! Okay?"

"Okay," he says. He sounds a little happier now. His true companion is on the way. Hopefully.

"I'm going to hide so the princess doesn't see me." I look around. But where? Too bad there's no trapdoor.

"Go under the water," Frederic says. "That's the only hiding place."

What choice do I have?

I lower myself under the water. It feels like bathwater. Someone else's bathwater. Ew. The rest of my pj's get soaked immediately.

A shadow crosses the top of the well. I crouch all the way down so my knees are in my chest and just my face is above water.

Here we go.

* chapter Six *

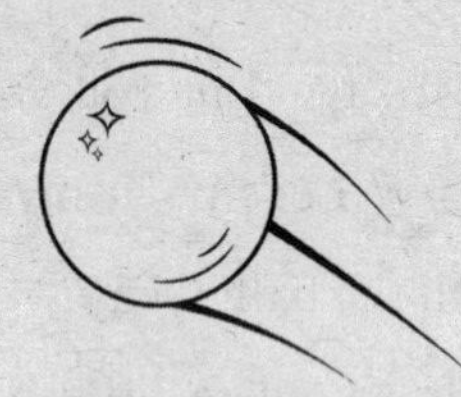

Great Catch

I hope it really is the princess. Otherwise, I am soaking myself in a disgusting well for no reason. I can't believe people actually drink this water.

"What a horribly hot day," a voice says from above. "And those useless guards still haven't added a bucket to the well like I demanded. How are we supposed to have a cool drink?"

It's a girl's voice. It must be the princess. But who is she talking to? Is she with someone? She's not with someone in the story.

"I could practice shooting arrows," she goes on. "But I didn't bring my bow. Oh, I know — I can work on catching with my left hand," she adds. "My left hand is so weak. I wish it were stronger."

"*Neigh!*" I hear. "*Neigh!*"

"I knew you'd agree," she says.

Oh! She's talking to her horse. I've done *that* before.

Suddenly, something gold goes flying through the air.

Yes! It really is her! It's the princess and that's her ball!

Up, up, up it goes. Is she going to catch it? Probably not if she's not great at catching with her left hand. Perfect!

"Now?" Frederic asks, his bulgy eyes watching the ball way up in the air.

"I hope so," I say. "The ball will drop in the water and you'll grab it."

We both watch the ball. I'm holding my breath. Come on. Come on.

Down, down, down it goes.

The princess's hand shoots out across the well opening and she catches it.

I have to admit, it was an impressive catch. Especially if she's a righty and that was her left hand. But suddenly, the ball is back up in the air again. Up, up, up it goes! It's really high! And down, down, down . . .

She catches it again!

Okay, here we go. Third time's the charm in fairy tales. It always is . . .

Up, up, up . . . and . . .

She catches it *again*.

ARGH. Are we going to be here all day?

Here it comes one more time. Up, up, up! It's higher this time! I think this is the one! It's coming down now. She's reaching for it! But I don't think she's going to be able to catch it. She's sticking out her hand as far as it will go, but the golden ball is too far over. She's going to miss it! The ball is going to plummet into the well!

Here we go, here it comes —

RUFF!

A shock of brown fur leaps across the air.

It grabs the golden ball in its mouth.

Huh?

What just happened? What was that?

Ohhhhhh.

The shock of fur was Prince. My dog just leaped across the well and caught the golden ball in his mouth.

The ball is not going to drop into the well.

The frog is not going to catch it.

Prince just totally messed up the story.

I don't know whether to cry or laugh. I settle on a small chuckle. It *is* kind of funny. Prince LOVES to play catch.

Then I shake my head in dismay. We ALWAYS mess up the story. What is wrong with us?

Then I laugh again. I can't help it.

"What's so funny?" Frederic asks me, forehead creased in confusion.

"Nothing," I whisper. The little frog looks so worried. Suddenly, Prince leaping to catch the ball doesn't seem so hilarious.

"Is the princess going to drop the ball now?" Frederic asks.

"Um . . . no," I admit. I'm about to tell him that we'll figure something out when the princess's screams interrupt me.

"Let go of my ball, you disgusting creature!" she yells.

Excuse me? Is she talking about my adorable, definitely not disgusting dog?

"Give it to me right this second, you miserable mutt, or you will be punished!" she yells.

Exqueeeeeeze me? Nobody punishes my dog but me. I don't even punish my dog! He's a good dog! A perfect gentleman. A perfect gentle*dog*. He doesn't need to be punished. He just saved her ball from falling in the well. She should be thankful!

"Give the ball back, Prince," I hear Jonah say.

I guess my brother is no longer hiding.

"Good dog," Jonah says.

Seems like Prince gave the princess back her ball. She'd better say thank you.

"Ew," the princess says. "You got my ball all slobbery! Gross! You're a disgusting animal. Bad dog! Bad dog!"

I feel like I'm going to explode. That's it. THAT'S IT! No one calls Prince a bad dog. No one! I stand up to my full height, water dripping off my pajamas.

"STOP BEING MEAN TO MY DOG!" I yell.

The princess peeks her head over the top off the well. She has short, choppy blond hair. She's also wearing a tiara. "Is someone down there?" she asks.

"Yes," I say. "I am. And I want you to apologize to Prince this instant!"

"Prince? What prince?"

Our dog's name tends to cause confusion when we visit fairy tales. Once, we even had to call an actual human prince Pickles to avoid confusing our adorable mutt. Not mutt. *Gentledog.*

"My dog is named Prince," I explain, scowling up at the princess. "And his behavior is a lot more royal than yours, missy! You were very rude!"

She snorts. "I am not apologizing to a *dog*. That's ridiculous. He slobbered all over my ball! It's *gold*. You can't slobber on gold."

"Your ball was about to fall into the well," I remind her. "You should be *thanking* him!"

The princess crinkles her nose. "No, I shouldn't! Why are you in the well anyway?"

"It's a long story," I say with a sigh. "Do you think you could help me get out?" I probably shouldn't have yelled at her before asking for a favor. But it's not like she's going to leave me here, right? I'm a girl stuck in a well.

The princess squints her eyes at me. She scrunches up her face, then lifts her chin. "You're wearing dirty pajamas!" she says. "Why would I help you? I'm Princess Cassandra. And you were spying on me. I'm not going to help you."

"You're not?" I ask. "Really?"

"Really!"

"But . . . but. . . ."

She laughs. "But nothing. I don't want to help you, so I won't. I want to eat lunch."

"Wait," Jonah calls. "Don't go!"

I hear a pitter-patter of hooves. I think it's too late. I think she left.

She left!

She left me in the well!

What kind of nasty princess is she? I should have known she wouldn't be the nicest princess of all time. After all, she *is* the princess who went back on her promise to the frog, and *then* threw the poor frog against a wall.

But still. I can't believe she left me IN THE WELL. Princess Cassandra is not very nice at all!

Jonah peeks his head over the edge. "What a meanie!"

"Awful!" I agree.

Poor Frederic. Where is he? He's being quiet. I glance around and don't see him. He's probably hiding because he's so upset. He's so sweet and nice. I can't believe he's going to have to marry the mean princess! And spend his whole life with her! Who knows what happens after the wedding in the fairy tale? The princess is probably horrible to him!

"Jonah," I say. "Maybe this is one of those times when the bad people *shouldn't* get rewarded."

"What do you mean?" my brother asks.

My heart starts to race. "I mean, maybe this is one of the times when we should try to mess up the story . . . on purpose."

Jonah's eyes open wide. "Really?" he asks.

"Really," I say, jumping in my flip-flops. "Of course I *want* Frederic to turn back into a prince. He's unhappy being a frog. But maybe he doesn't have to marry the princess. Maybe we don't need the princess at all. Maybe we can change him back on our own!"

"Yeah!" Jonah cries.

"Yeah!" I echo. "Right, Frederic?" I ask, looking around again. "What do you think? We don't need the horrible princess, do we?" There's no answer. "Frederic?" I call again. I peer down into the water and up around the walls of the well. I don't see him. "Mr. Frog Prince? Where are you?"

No answer.

"Frederic!" I squat down to feel around. I touch nothing but water. There is no frog.

The frog prince is gone.

* chapter Seven *

Hop to It

"He must have jumped out!" I yelp. "Did you see him leave?"

"No!" Jonah says. "But I wasn't paying complete attention."

Can frogs climb? I think they can! Yes — their little feet can be like suction cups and stick to surfaces. "He must have climbed up the wall and hopped away while the princess was being mean to me! But why would he do that?" Argh!

"Now what?" Jonah asks.

I frown. "Now I *really* have to get out of the well. We have to find that frog! Jonah, are you *sure* there's no rope or bucket there?"

"I'm sure."

"Is there anything else you can use to pull me up?"

"Maybe . . . a branch?" he asks. "From one of the giant *Jack and the Beanstalk* trees?"

I snort-laugh. "Okay. Go get a branch!"

"Be right back!"

Luckily, my brother is an excellent tree climber. He disappears and a few minutes later, he dangles a very long branch down the well. The branch is brown and rough with some smaller, skinnier branches and lots of leaves. I'm not sure what I'm supposed to hold on to exactly.

"Those trees are really huge," Jonah says. "And I think I saw a monkey!"

"Great. Just get me out!"

"And guess what!" he adds, scratching his head. "I had another Maryrose memory!"

"A helpful one? Like maybe Maryrose once had to find a missing, talking frog and found him in . . ." I look at my brother expectantly, hoping he'll fill in the blank, Mad Libs–style.

"When Maryrose was a kid," Jonah says instead, "she loved to eat bananas. Seeing the monkeys made me remember!"

Argh. More totally useless information. "Okay, then. Good to know. Let's focus on getting me out of here."

"Hold on to the branch and climb!" Jonah instructs.

"But how?" I ask. "There are too many leaves!"

"Wait! Itchy head!" Jonah shouts. "I need to scratch! Ah, that's better. Okay, grab the branch!"

"Take these!" I say and throw him my flip-flops.

"You're wearing shoes?" he asks.

"Yes!"

"Why didn't you bring me shoes?"

"I'm sorry, I was in a rush! Can we discuss this once you get me out, please?"

He holds the branch steady for me and I grab hold. I slip a few times, but I climb slowly and finally make it up. I grab hold of the top of the well, and Jonah pulls me over the edge.

"Ahhhh," I say as my feet finally touch dry ground. "We did it."

I blink in all the sunlight. It's hot out. As horribly hot as the princess said it was. And muggy. It was much cooler in the well. My soaking-wet pajamas are sticking to me even more now. Jonah hands me back my flip-flops and I slip them on.

I look around and try to get my bearings. There's a long road that the princess must have ridden her horse down. We're in a clearing where she had probably been tossing her ball. It's surrounded by trees. Huge trees like Jonah said. Not exactly beanstalks, but I see where he was coming from. The trees are about a hundred feet high and at least five feet wide. All around me, birds are chirping. A black, yellow, and red one swoops next to me. Oh! It looks like the toucan on the Froot Loops box, with its long, curved beak.

I think we're in a tropical forest!

The sun is certainly hot enough. I can see it through the leaves, smack in the middle of the sky. I guess that means it's middle of the day here? Noon? One? Something like that? I glance at my watch. It's twelve twenty in the morning at home. Since we left at midnight, that means that only twenty minutes have passed at home. Since I was in the well for at least an hour, that means time passes faster here than it does it Smithville. Maybe three times as fast? My parents wake us up at seven. So we have six hours and forty minutes of Smithville time before we need to be home. If you multiply that by three . . . that's twenty hours. We have twenty hours to stay in this fairy tale. That's enough time, right?

"Frederic!" I call out. "Where did you go?"

No reply. No croaky little voice. Only the sound of birds chirping.

"Froggy!" I call out again. "Here, froggy froggy!" Where could he be? I turn to Jonah. "Where would he go?"

Prince barks. Then he pants. He must be thirsty. Poor doggie, doggie.

"Frogs like the water," Jonah says, rubbing Prince's head.

"But he just left the well," I remind him. "There was water in there."

Jonah thinks for a second. "Maybe he went to find other water. Fresher water that doesn't have people in it."

Good point. "Maybe. But where is the other water?" I don't see any water anywhere around, only trees. "Can you climb back up the tree and look around?"

"Definitely!" Jonah says. "Give me a sec. You should come up with me, Abby. There's a ton of huge birds in there!"

"I'll take your word for it," I say. "I've done enough climbing for one day."

Jonah scrunches up his face and then grabs hold of a tree.

The trunk is really tall, but it takes him only two minutes to climb up. Prince barks, cheering him on. Jonah disappears inside the leaves, and I can't see him anymore. "Jonah? You okay?" I yell. “You haven’t gotten eaten by one of the Froot Loops birds have you?”

“No!” he calls down. “I’m okay!”

“Can you see anything?”

“Yes! Hey, I see a black horse-drawn carriage. Maybe the princess is inside.”

“Wasn’t the princess just on horseback?” I ask.

“Oh, right,” Jonah says. “Maybe the princess’s parents are in the carriage.”

“Forget the princess and the carriage! We have to find Frederic. We can’t let him get away! We have to help him change back. He has to save his kingdom from his evil sister! We have to rescue the ten-year-olds she put in prison! Do you see water anywhere?” I ask.

“I see a stream over there!” Jonah says.

“Where’s there? I can’t see you!”

“There!”

I roll my eyes. I have no idea where *there* is. “Just make sure you know which direction we need to go in, and come down.”

A few minutes later, Jonah lands with a thud, and a smile on his face. “I saw a baby monkey! It was so cute!”

“Careful with the animals,” I warn.

"I was! I didn't touch it! Not really. Only its toe."

"Just lead the way."

Jonah points to the right, and I follow him down the path. Prince goes running ahead of us.

"So that girl wasn't Tiana?" Jonah asks as we walk.

"No. Tiana didn't start out as a princess," I remind him.

"But does kissing a princess change the frog back in the real story?"

"No," I say again. "In the Grimm version, the princess throws the frog against the wall and that's what changes him into a prince."

"Ouch."

"Yeah. But there are lots of versions of the story. In the Disney movie, a kiss undoes the curse. Well, first a kiss turns Tiana into a frog, but then a kiss also undoes it. In some versions, the frog has to sleep on the princess's pillow." I smile. I know my brother will like the next one. "And in other versions, the princess has to chop off the frog's head!"

His eyes light up. "NO WAY!"

"Way," I say. My brother is not as familiar as I am with the fairy tales. He never really paid attention when our nana read them to us. Since we found the magic mirror in the basement,

I've been rereading a lot of the tales to better prepare myself for our adventures. Jonah has not. He's been climbing trees.

Good thing both our interests have come in handy today.

We continue walking. The forest is quiet and not quiet at the same time. I can hear birds making all kinds of chirps and caws.

"There it is," Jonah says a few minutes later. "Yay! I took us the right way."

In front of us is a small stream of blue-green-brown water. The stream isn't very wide but is moving fast over rocks. And who is sitting on one of the rocks?

A frog! A frog with the same brown spots and regal posture!

"There he is!" I say.

I give Jonah a well-deserved high five.

"Frederic!" I say. "Hi! We need to talk to you!"

Frederic jumps onto another rock.

"No, wait," I tell him. "Don't be afraid of us. We have an idea."

Instead of answering, he hops off the rock and leaps into the stream.

"No, Frederic, come back!" I shout.

But he ignores me, hopping from rock to tiny rock in the water. Both sides of the stream are lined by the huge trees and all kinds of colorful flowers. What if he disappears into the tropical forest? We'll never find him. We have to help him! If we don't, he could be stuck as a frog forever. Prince messed up the story, and now Frederic is our responsibility! The fate of the entire kingdom of Frogville is our responsibility!

"Wait," Jonah calls to him. He runs along the shore in the direction Frederic is going. "Stop!"

I start running, too. So does Prince. But the faster we run, the faster Frederic leaps. He's leaping from rock to rock to rock, and he's faster than we are. And the stream is getting wider! He's getting away from us!

"Look!" Jonah says. "A boat!" Up ahead is a small, rusty canoe. "Let's take that!"

"Perfect," I say. I'm not sure why there is a random boat abandoned there, but who am I to say no to a canoe? Not that I've ever been in a canoe before. But how hard can it be?

I step inside and Prince jumps in beside me.

"I'll push us out," Jonah says. He shoves the canoe farther into the water. And then . . . we're moving! Jonah runs through the water and jumps behind me into the boat.

We're canoeing! We are on our way!

We're going down the stream! Hurrah! We're coming, Frederic, we're coming!

Wait. We're missing something. Something very important.

"Jonah?" I ask as we zip along the stream. "Where are the paddles?"

"Paddles?" he repeats.

"Yes. Paddles. To steer the canoe."

"We don't need paddles," he says. "We're moving on our own. We're about to catch Frederic. I see him right over —" Jonah looks at the rocks again. "Hey, where is he?" He bites his lip, squinting. "There he is!" Jonah shouts. "He's sitting on that big grayish-brownish-whitish rock up ahead. I'm going to reach out and grab him when we get up to him. Hold my legs!"

The canoe is moving fast. But if Jonah can reach Frederic, we'll have our froggy friend in the boat with us in a second.

"Now!" Jonah says, sticking out his arms.

"Careful, Jonah, careful!" I hold my brother's legs tight as he reaches over to grab Frederic. Prince barks and leans over the side of the boat, too.

"Almost got him . . . almost got him . . . I got him!" Jonah calls out. He uses both hands to catch Frederic and holds tight.

"Don't squash him!" I yell.

Jonah leans back into the boat, his hands cupped in front of him. "I'm not," Jonah says. He opens his fingers. "Hi, Frederic! It's us. Don't be afraid. We're here to help."

Frederic just stares.

Wait a minute. This frog is smaller than I remember. More of a brownish color, not so green. And his eyes aren't as bulgy. I stare at the frog. Didn't Frederic have more spots on him?

"Jonah, are we sure this is Frederic?" I ask.

"Huh?" my brother says.

Oh, right. Jonah didn't see Frederic up close like I did.

Prince sniffs the frog for a second, causing Frederic to freeze in fear.

"Don't scare him!" I tell Prince.

I bend down to study the frog in Jonah's hand. The spots are similar . . . but not exactly the same. And maybe all frogs have regal posture?

"I don't think this frog is Frederic." I say.

Jonah stares at the frog. "Oops. How do we know for sure?"

"Are you Frederic?" I ask the frog. "Say something if you are!"

The frog looks at both of us. *"Ribbit?"* he asks in a croak.

"He can't talk!" I cry. "It's *not* Frederic! Frederic can talk!"

"Is he even a frog?" Jonah asks. "He might be a toad."

"What's the difference?"

"I'm not sure. I think toads are wartier. And this guy is pretty warty."

"Great. Just great," I say.

"What do I do with him?" Jonah asks, still holding the frog/toad gingerly in his palms.

"Let him go," I order.

Jonah holds his hands out toward the water. "Jump, froggy, jump!"

The frog/toad that is not Frederic doesn't jump. He just sits, big-eyed, looking terrified.

Which is understandable, considering how fast we're going in the canoe. I can hear the wind whistling through my hair. My stomach lurches. Prince sticks his neck out of the boat, enjoying the breeze in his face.

"Um, Jonah, how do we stop this thing if we don't have paddles?" I ask nervously.

"Aren't there brakes?" Jonah asks.

"DO YOU SEE BRAKES?" I yell.

The frog/toad that is not Frederic starts to quake at my very loud voice.

"Abby!" Jonah says. "I just remembered something!"

Jonah has that strange look on his face. He must have another of Maryrose's memories. Probably that she once sang a lullaby on a windy day. OR SOMETHING ELSE TOTALLY USELESS. "Is it about canoeing?" I ask, trying to be positive.

He scratches his head. "It is! Maryrose was good at canoeing!"

Oh! Yay! "Did she ever stop a boat?"

"Yes!" he exclaims.

Great! "How?" I ask.

"With paddles!" he says.

Argh. "Thanks for nothing, Maryrose's memories!" I yell. "We have to stop this canoe!"

We're going faster and faster down the stream now. The water around us is getting choppier and choppier. I reach out to grip the sides of the boat. There are no handles. There are no seat belts.

There is NO way to stop the canoe.

"I've always wanted to go white-water rafting!" Jonah exclaims.

"I haven't!" I shout. I am not really a fan of the water. "Especially not without life jackets."

"I'm sure the water will slow down soon," Jonah says, but he doesn't sound convinced.

I hold on tight. Very tight. And then I see it.

Up ahead. There's a drop. The water dives down.

It's a waterfall. Seriously?

"Brace yourself!" I shout over the sound of the rushing water. Prince howls.

We are heading straight for it. The canoe is moving faster! And faster!

I scream as we sail right over the edge.

* chapter eight *

Pucker Up

"Ahhhhhhh!" we shout. My stomach swoops.

Cold water rains down on us as we go over. It feels like we're taking the biggest shower EVER. Water goes in my nose. A lot of it.

The boat lands at the bottom of the falls and then capsizes. Jonah and I fall out, and are suddenly upside down and underwater. Somehow, miraculously, my flip-flops stay on my feet as I swim to the surface.

I pop my head above the water, sputtering and pushing my wet hair out of my eyes. Prince doggie-paddles up next to me, his fur soaked. He's okay. We're okay.

I look around in every direction. Oh, no. Where is my brother?

"Jonah!" I yell.

I don't see him anywhere.

My heart thumps. "Jonah!" I yell, and Prince starts barking. "Where are you?" I cry.

"Right here!"

I blink. My brother is on the other side of the upside-down canoe, as soaking wet as I am.

PHEW!

"I'm fine," he assures me. "That was *fun*! Can we do it again?"

"No," I say simply, trying to catch my breath while treading water. Is he crazy? I'd call what we just did a lot of things, but definitely not fun.

Okay, maybe a tiny bit fun. Also a tiny bit refreshing. Okay, a lot refreshing. What can I say? This kingdom is HOT.

I grab hold of the other side of the canoe. "Where did the not-Frederic frog go?" I ask. "Is he okay?"

"He must've jumped away," Jonah says.

I look around as we bob in the water. We're in some sort of lagoon, surrounded by more gigantic trees. The water on this side of the falls is much calmer and not too deep.

"Are you guys okay?" someone asks.

The voice came from a lily pad near the shore.

It came from a frog. A frog doing push-ups.

Could there be more than one talking frog? And would your average frog be doing push-ups?

"Frederic!" I call out. "Is that you?"

"It's me," he shouts back. "Forty-nine," he says, doing another push-up, his little green froggy legs stretched out straight to support his full weight. He bends his legs, lowering his belly to the ground. "And fifty! Done!" He wipes his forehead with his little leg. "Sorry. I need to keep in shape," he adds.

Yay! We found him! I've never been so happy to see an exercising frog in my life. Also I realize that being bigger, greener, and having bulgy eyes and lots of spots aren't the only differences between the frog/toad and Frederic.

Frederic is wearing shorts.

Shorts! Brown ones! How did I miss that?

I guess they blended into the background of the well.

"We've been looking for you," I tell Frederic, swimming toward him. Jonah follows close behind, and Prince does as well. "Where did you go?" I ask our froggy friend.

Frederic glances at me sheepishly. “I tried to follow the princess. But she got away. She was too fast on her horse again.” He sighs. “I don’t think she would have helped me.”

“I’m not sure she would have, either,” I admit, reaching the shore. “She didn’t seem very nice. Sorry about that. But don’t worry,” I add. “I have a new plan. We don’t need that princess. We don’t need *any* princess.”

“We don’t?” Frederic hops toward me. “Hey. Are you a fairy?”

“No,” I tell him. “But I’m going to turn you human.”

His eyes bulge even more than normal. “You are?”

“Yes!

“How?”

“I’ll tell you in a second,” I say. I step out of the water, Jonah at my side and Prince at my heels, all three of us completely soaked. My flip-flops make squishing sounds on the ground. I yank a section of my flannel pajama bottoms away from my leg and it plasters right back to my skin. Jonah looks like he took a bath in *his* pajamas. Prince gives himself a big hearty shake and water flies everywhere.

Frederic hops onto a big rock so he’s up higher.

"So how are you going to change me?" he asks.

I wring out my wet hair and push it back behind my shoulders. "There are a few things we can try," I say.

"How do you know?" he asks.

"Where I come from, there's a story called *The Frog Prince*."

Frederic looks really happy suddenly. "*I'm* the frog prince!" he says, puffing up his little green chest.

"I know. Anyway, there are many versions of the story. And you always change back to your human form by the end, but the way it happens is always different."

"Great!" he cries. "Let's try. What's the best one?"

"Well, the Grimm one might hurt, so let's start with the more popular one. In that version, the princess kisses the frog. Right after the kiss, the frog changes back."

"Okay, then!" Frederic says. "Let's try that. Kiss me, Abby!"

Jonah cracks up. "I thought you said no one is kissing anyone, Abby. You're really going to kiss a frog? You're not even a princess!"

I scowl at my brother. "Yes, Jonah. I'm going to kiss a frog. And I bet it doesn't matter that I'm not a princess. It's the act of kindness — a human kissing a frog even though he's a frog — that matters."

Jonah is bent over in laughter.

"Are you going to kiss him on the lips?" he squeals.

I give Frederic a close inspection. "I was thinking on the nose," I say.

"But what about what happens in the movie?" Jonah asks. "Didn't Tiana turn into a frog after she kissed the frog? What if *you* turn into a frog?"

"That only happened in the movie," I say. "We are not in the movie! Does this look like the city of New Orleans? No, it does not."

I hold my hand out, palm up, in front of Frederic. "Come on up."

He jumps onto my hand, and I lift him up. "Ready?" I ask.

I am going to kiss a frog. I am about to kiss a frog!

I better *not* turn into a frog.

"Ready!" he exclaims. He stretches out his nose.

I lean over. His nose and lips are pretty much all the same. I pucker my lips and give him a quick peck.

Honestly? Kissing a frog isn't so awful. Frederic isn't *that* slimy. His skin feels like regular skin that's just coated in something slimy. Like Vaseline. And he smells like . . . nothing, really. Maybe he smells a little bit like the bottom of a lake. Or a well.

I pull back.

Oh! Hey! I did not turn into a frog!

I put Frederic back on the ground.

Unfortunately, he still *is* a frog. I should give it a few seconds, right? Maybe some crazy purple swirl is going on in his body that I can't see. Maybe any second now, he'll morph from a six-inch-tall amphibian to a six-foot-tall prince.

I tilt my head and look closely at him to see if anything's changing.

Nothing happens. He doesn't turn into a prince. He is still small. He is still green. He is still a frog.

CRUMBS.

"Did it work?" Frederic asks.

I have to give him the bad news. "No," I say.

"Try again!" he orders. Frederick sure can be bossy sometimes. But hey, I get it. I'd be bossy, too, if I got turned into a frog and had to depend on someone else to turn me back.

I try again. Another peck on the nose/lips. It still doesn't work.

"Jonah, you try," Frederic says.

"Gross," Jonah says, wrinkling up his face. "I don't want to kiss a frog."

"Jonah!" I command. "Kiss the frog!"

Jonah takes a step back, crossing his arms over his chest. "Why would it work if I kiss him but not if you kiss him? Neither of us are princesses."

"I don't know! But we might as well try it. C'mon!"

Jonah groans. Then he leans over to Frederic, who is still in my hand. "Hello. Nice to meet you up close."

"Hello," Frederic says. His bulging eyes are so hopeful.

Please work, please work.

A shadow crosses Jonah's face. "Hmm. There's something familiar about you."

"About me?" Frederic asks.

"Yeah." Jonah looks confused. He scratches his head. Twice. He squints his eyes at Frederic and bites his lower lip.

"Didn't you have a stuffed frog when you were a kid?" I ask.

Frederic gasps. "You stuffed a frog?"

"A stuffed animal frog," I say quickly. "It was a toy. Which he loved. He named it Ribbit! Nana got it for him for Hanukkah one year." I turn back to my brother. "Maybe Frederic reminds you of Ribbit."

"Maybe," Jonah says, scratching again above his ear.

He must be having a Maryrose memory. "Or maybe our fairy friend had a pet frog?" I offer.

Frederic hops on his froggy toes. "You have a fairy friend? Can she help us?"

"Unfortunately, she's not here," I say. "Just her memories are."

"Huh?" Frederic asks.

"Not important," I say, with a wave of my hand. "Jonah, can you get on with it? We don't have all day."

The frog has to turn human soon so we can get home before Mom and Dad wake up. I give my watch a fast glance. It's now one A.M. back home.

Jonah quickly kisses Frederic on the nose/lips. "There. Happy? That better work."

It doesn't. Frederic is still a frog.

"Let the dog try," Frederic begs.

"Really?" I ask skeptically. "Prince?"

Frederic nods. "Yes. Why not? Dog! Come here!"

I guess so. Prince's kisses have been magical before. And his *name* is royal. "Prince! Come!" I call.

Prince runs over, tail wagging.

"Can you give the frog a kiss?" I ask him. Prince always seems to understand me.

Ruff, ruff, ruff! he replies, wagging his tail even more.

Prince towers over Frederic, and Frederic takes a leap back. possibly reconsidering. "He's not going to eat me, is he?"

"I don't think so," I say. "You won't eat Frederic, right, Prince?"

Ruff.

I hope that's a no.

I point Prince toward Frederic. Prince sticks out his tongue and licks the entire side of Frederic's body, drenching Frederic in dog slobber.

"Enough, enough!" Frederic cries, scowling. "It's not working. Get him off!"

I pull Prince away. "Thanks, Princey."

"Now what?" Frederic asks. "We're out of people."

"And animals," Jonah adds. "We should probably ask the princess. That's who's *supposed* to turn him back into a human."

"We're not asking the princess!" I snap. "We don't need her. We should try throwing Frederic against the wall, anyway. That's what worked in the Grimm story."

"Oh, boy," Frederic says. "That *does* sound grim."

Hah. That was funny although he probably doesn't get the joke.

Jonah's eyes brighten. "Let's try that! Let's throw him against a wall!"

I stare at my brother. "You were squeamish about the kissing but have no problem throwing a frog against a wall?"

He cocks his head to the side. "Why would I have a problem throwing a frog against a wall?"

"You wouldn't. You're weird." I look around the forest. "Anyway, there is no wall anywhere around here."

"Can we throw him against a tree?" Jonah asks, pointing at the closest one.

I wince. "Sounds painful."

"No more painful than throwing me against a wall," Frederic argues. "Just do it! I want you to."

"All right," I say and pick Frederic up. I find the closest tree and raise my arm.

Frederic's whole body tenses.

Now.

Okay now.

Really this time.

"What's the problem?" Frederic asks, looking up at me.

"I can't throw you against a tree!" I cry. "I'm sorry! I can't do it!"

"You have to!" Frederic insists.

"I'll do it," Jonah calls out. "I don't mind."

I pass Frederic to him. "Not too hard," I remind him.

"Ready?" Jonah asks.

"Ready!" Frederic says, but I can see his small frog body scrunching up.

Jonah rolls his arm back like he's throwing a baseball. Then he suddenly stops. "Hey," he says. "I think there's someone behind that tree."

Frederic stretches his neck to look. "I don't see anyone."

"Me neither," I say, glancing around the trunk.

"I'm pretty sure I saw someone with a blue hat on," Jonah insists.

"I'll go check it out," Frederic says, taking a flying leap over to the tree. He disappears behind it, then hops back over to us. "No, no one there. No one at all. There's a tall plant with a blue flower at the top. Maybe you saw that?"

"Yeah, probably," Jonah says, holding out his hand. Frederic jumps onto his palm. "Okay. Back to business!" Jonah says as he winds up his arm. "On your mark. Get set. Let's go!"

I clench. This is going to hurt.

Jonah throws and Frederic flies in an arc across the sky.

"Ahhhhh!" Frederic screams. His arms and legs are spread-eagled and pointed in all directions and he's headed right toward the tree.

I can't watch! I slam my eyes shut.

Smash!

I open my eyes again and go running toward the tree. Frederic is on the ground in an awkward position. "Are you okay?" I call out.

"Maybe," he squeaks. "Did I change back into a human?"

How much bad news do I have to give the poor little guy? "No," I tell him. "Still a frog."

He groans.

"Sorry," I say.

"Maybe it can't be a tree," Jonah points out. "Maybe it has to be an actual wall. Like it was in the story."

I glance around. Trees, trees, and more trees. "No walls here."

"Well, then we'll find a wall," Frederic says.

Okay, either this frog likes slamming into hard surfaces or he really, really, really wants to be human again. I'm going with option two. "You want my brother to throw you again?"

Frederic nods. "If that's what it takes, then yes!"

"Let's go to the palace," Jonah says. "I saw it when I climbed the tree. It's not too far that way," he adds, pointing toward the path.

I grind my teeth. "I told you, I don't want to get the princess involved. She's horrible. We don't need her."

"We don't have to get her involved," my brother says. "There's a wall around the palace."

Frederic slurps up a fly with his tongue. "Then let's go!"

I consider what Jonah said. "Wait. You could see the palace when you climbed the tree?"

Jonah nods. "Yup."

I narrow my eyes at my brother. "Does that mean you could see the waterfall, too?"

"Yup!"

"Jonah!"

"What?" he asks sheepishly. "It was fun."

I shake my head. "Lead the way," I say, and he does.

* chapter nine *

Jonah Bologna

We walk for over an hour. The frog hops onto Jonah's scrawny shoulder, passing the time by doing push-ups. He counts to a hundred, takes a break, and starts again. I can probably do ten push-ups, maybe eleven, max. In a day.

I wish I had someone to carry me on his shoulder. The branches on the forest floor keep scraping my ankles. At least I'm wearing shoes, unlike my brother. I try to give him mine but he says walking in too big flip-flops is even harder than being barefoot.

The sun lowers in the sky, and my watch says it's one-thirty at home.

"There it is!" Jonah exclaims. He points at the castle looming right in front of us in a huge clearing in the forest.

"And it does have a wall!" Frederic says from where he's sitting on Jonah's shoulder. "Throw me, throw me!"

We walk closer to the wall that surrounds the palace, careful to stay behind a block of trees. The wall is dark brown and kind of rough instead of smooth stone, like castle walls usually are. I squint to see better. Oh! It's wood. I guess that's what happens when your kingdom has lots of huge trees. The wood has carvings of birds etched into it. Right in the center of the wall is an arched opening. To the side of the opening is a guard.

He is round, bald, and fast asleep in a rocking chair. He's wearing a gold uniform with an insignia of three different kinds of birds on his chest. In script above the birds is the word *BIRDOPOLIS*.

Birdopolis. Maybe that's the name of the kingdom. That would explain the bird etchings. And there sure are a lot of birds around here.

"He looks comfortable," Jonah comments. The guard lets out a snore and his double chin wiggles against his chest.

"Good," I whisper. "Nobody wake him!" I glance over at

Prince, who's busy chasing a white butterfly in circles. "Prince, remember to be very quiet."

Prince stops and looks at me. Not a woof. Not a ruff. Then he goes back to chasing the butterfly. Good boy!

See that, horrible princess? Prince *is* a good dog! "Let's move around to the side," I say. "So we'll be out of sight."

We move over to the left side of the wall. No arched openings or sleeping guards. Just a lot of wood.

Frederic looks at my brother with his big, frog eyes. "Do it here," he says. "Throw me against this wall."

Jonah's face lights up again. "Will do," he says. He scoops up the frog. "Should I throw you superfast?"

"Whatever it takes," Frederic mutters.

"Here goes," Jonah says, winding his arm back with Frederic cupped in his hand.

But just before he lets go, he freezes, his eye catching on something in the distance. "Hey, there's the carriage I saw when I was up in the tree." He points a few feet away. A horse-drawn carriage — a fancy black one — is stopped on the path behind some giant trees. There's a driver there, but he's too far away for me to see him clearly.

The driver seems to notice we're watching him. He cracks the reins on the horse and gallops away.

"He definitely saw us," Jonah says. "Is he going to tell the guards on us? Do you think he's security?"

"Well, he's driving away from the palace, so I guess not," I point out.

"Forget all that!" Frederic yelps. "I have an appointment with this wall! Throw me!"

Jonah pulls his arm back, and Frederic once again goes flying through the air.

Slam. His froggy body hits the wall with a thud.

I wince. Poor Frederic!

But was being thrown against the wall worth it? Is he about to turn into a prince?

I hold my breath.

And . . . nada.

No prince. Frederic the frog slides down the wall to the ground with a splat.

"Argh! I'm still a frog, aren't I?" Frederic croaks. He sounds miserable.

He's probably getting scared he'll never change back.

"Sorry," I tell him. "Still a frog."

Frederic sighs and hops over to us. Then he snaps a bug into his mouth with his tongue. "Disgusting," he says.

I think about how many bugs and other insects Frederic has to have eaten since he became a frog. "I bet you can't wait to be human again. And have a burger."

"With fries, not flies," Jonah adds.

I laugh.

"Do you know I ate frog legs once?" Jonah asks.

Uh-oh.

"You *what*?" screams a horrified Frederic.

"It's true!" Jonah says, clearly not catching the *stop talking* look I'm shooting him. "We went to a French restaurant for our dad's birthday and he ordered an appetizer of frog legs. Remember, Abby? We tried them! Both of us did!"

"It was before I knew you," I tell Frederic apologetically.

"They tasted like chicken!" Jonah exclaims.

He's right. They did taste like chicken.

"I think I'm going to throw up," Frederic moans.

"We won't eat your legs," I say. "Or your arms. We won't eat any part of you. We promise!"

"Humph." Frederic crosses his arms over his chest and clucks his tongue.

"Let's focus on making you human again," I say, trying to change the subject.

"Maybe we should try a wall *inside* the castle," Jonah suggests. "Maybe the wall has to be an actual palace wall."

"And risk running into the Princess Cassandra?" I ask. "No way. She's evil! Who knows what she'll do if she catches us!"

"Maybe she'll throw Frederic against the wall and that will change him back?"

"No!"

"If you have better ideas, feel free to share them," Jonah says.

"Well, there are *other* versions of the story," I say, thinking out loud. "Besides the throwing and the kissing."

"Like what?" Frederic asks.

I bite my lip. This is going to be worse than the frog-legs conversation.

"Well, there's the one where the princess chops off the frog's head, and then he turns into a prince," I say all in a rush.

Frederic's eyes almost pop out of his head. "I do not wish to try that one."

Jonah snort-laughs. "I wouldn't, either."

"It is a little risky," I admit. "Okay. We should skip it."

"Are there any versions that don't require an ax?" Frederic asks with a gulp.

"Yes!" I say. "There's one where the frog falls asleep on the princess's pillow and when she wakes him, he's a human prince again."

"That doesn't sound too painful," Frederic says. Then he yawns. "It actually sounds quite pleasant. And I could use a nap. I've been leaping around all day. You have no idea how exhausting being an amphibian is."

"But how are we going to get Princess Cassandra's pillow?" Jonah asks. "We *have* to go inside the castle for that."

I pout. Why would I want to ever lay eyes on that horrible princess again after what she said and did to me? She left me in a well! Knee-deep in water! Smelly water! She's worse than Brandon the bully!

And that's really bad.

"We have to," Frederic echoes. "We need a princess's pillow. And we're right in front of a castle. Where a princess lives. One plus one equals two."

I stomp my foot. "I hate that we have to go in."

"I can go alone," Frederic says.

"No way. It's our responsibility to help you. I just hate that we need that meanie's pillow." I stomp my foot again.

"Don't be crabby, Abby," Jonah says.

I narrow my eyes. "Didn't I tell you not to call me that?"

He bats his eyelashes innocently. "You did?"

Frederic snorts. "Crabby Abby?"

"No one's allowed to call me that!"

"Now you're really sounding like a crab, Ab," Jonah says.

I stick out my tongue. "Would you like it if I called you Jonah . . . Bologna?"

He cracks up. "Jonah Bologna? Yes, I *would* like it if you called me Jonah Bologna — I would like to eat some Jonah Bologna. It sounds delicious. Can I put ketchup on it?"

Why didn't I see that coming? Of course Jonah would want to be called Jonah Bologna. "Hmph. Never mind." I turn my back to him.

We hear a voice. A girl's voice, coming from behind the wall. "I'm leaving again!" she calls out. "Taking my horse! See you in the morning! Not that anyone's listening!"

It's Princess Cassandra!

"Hide," I whisper to the others. "We don't want her to see us."

Frederic hops onto Jonah's shoulder. We press our backs against the wall, out of sight. I kneel down and hold a squirming Prince in my arms. Who knows what would happen if Prince ran over to her?

"Morton? Are you napping again? Great security we have here," the princess mutters sarcastically as she rides off on her horse.

Morton, the guard, snort-snores. He readjusts to a comfortable position before falling back asleep.

We wait until we're sure the princess is gone and Morton is really in dreamland. Then we all let out a big sigh of relief. I release Prince and get to my feet.

"This is perfect," Frederic says, hopping off Jonah's shoulder and onto the ground. His big eyes are lighting up. "Now we know for sure that the princess isn't home. Let's get onto her pillow!"

"Yeah," Jonah says. "And when we're in the palace, we should try throwing Frederic against a wall, too. Since we'll be in there anyway."

I ruffle my brother's hair. "You really do like the throwing part."

"You should try it! It's fun!"

I shudder. "I don't think I can." Throwing a cute little frog at a wall? No way. I can't even imagine throwing Brandon the bully at a wall. Okay, maybe I can.

"Can we go already?" Frederic asks, leaping from frog foot to frog foot. "We're wasting time."

He's right. We have to keep moving.

"Follow me," I say, motioning to Jonah and Frederic. "Quiet, Prince," I remind the dog. Then, on my tiptoes, I walk right past the sleeping guard's chair. Only a few more steps and we'll be inside the palace grounds.

"Worst guard ever!" Jonah whispers from behind me.

"Shush!" I whisper back.

"Okay, okay," Jonah says as quietly as he can. Then he tiptoes past the snoozing guard and through the opening.

Frederic takes a flying leap right inside.

Prince very quietly pads through next.

We're all in!

* chapter ten *

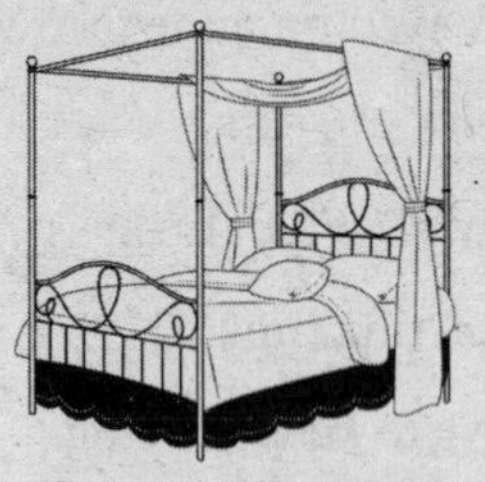

Coco's Room

The opening leads to a wooden walkway, which is about a football field away from the palace front door.

The walkway passes through the palace garden. On the left and right are trees and tropical-looking red and orange flowers.

The castle itself is made of wood, too, stained dark.

So much wood.

There's another guard blocking the front door. But this one is awake. He's scrawny, sitting on a chair and reading a newspaper.

"Let's go in," Jonah says.

"We can't just stroll through the front door," I say, pulling my brother over to the side where there are a cluster of trees. Two big, bright, striped birds with long beaks swoop over our heads and disappear around the side of the castle.

"I'll hop around the grounds and see if there's another way to get in," Frederic says, leaping through the grass.

He doesn't have to worry about being caught. No one would try and arrest him. You can't put a frog in prison. Lucky duck. Um . . . lucky frog.

We wait for him to come back. And wait some more. "Where is he?" I wonder out loud.

"What if someone stepped on him?" Jonah asks.

"Frederic is way too fast for that," I assure him. "Besides, no one's around."

"Except them," Jonah says, pointing to a family of monkeys hanging from one of the trees. "Monkeys are really smart, you know. And loyal. Maybe we can take one home as a pet?"

Prince barks. It sounds a little like *no way.*

Jonah takes a step toward them.

"Do not touch them, Jonah!"

He makes a sad face.

There's another moment of quiet and then —

"There he is!" Jonah whisper-shouts in my ear. "Frederic is coming back!"

Frederic leaps over to the tree we're hiding behind.

"What did you find out?" I ask him.

"There's a swimming pool in the back!" he exclaims, smiling. "With a slide and noodles!"

Jonah sighs. "I wish we could go swimming."

I frown at my brother. We're still damp from our little dip in the stream. "Seriously?" I ask. Jonah shrugs and smiles at me.

"There's also a door in the back," Frederic goes on. "But there's a guard there, too. He's sitting by the pool, having a tall frosty drink, and he's definitely awake." Frederic sighs.

"Maybe we can climb up the wall right into the princess's bedroom," Jonah suggests, gazing up at the tall castle.

"But we can't possibly know which one is her bedroom," I remind him. The castle is huge. Judging from the many windows, it looks like there are about twenty rooms on each floor and there are five floors.

"I bet it's that one on the side," Jonah says matter-of-factly, pointing up.

"How do you know?"

"Because there's a sign in that window that says Princess Coco. See?"

What?

He's right! Silver letters spelling out P-R-I-N-C-E-S-S C-O-C-O hang across the window.

"But her name is Cassandra," I say. "Not Coco."

"Cassandra is her real name. Coco is her nickname," Frederic says.

"Her nickname shouldn't be Princess Coco. It should be Princess *Cruel*."

"Let's climb up!" Jonah says, beckoning for us to follow him.

I look up at the five-story castle. "Jonah, it seems really high," I say. "I don't know." Prince whines and presses against my ankles, like he's hesitant, too. His little paws aren't made for climbing.

Someone clears his throat. "Ahem."

We all turn around. Morton, the round, bald, formerly sleeping guard, is standing in front of us. He yawns. He has a half-eaten apple in one hand.

GULP.

"You're Princess Coco's friends, right?" he asks.

Jonah and I look at each other.

"Um, yes!" I tell the guard. "We were playing ball with her by the well earlier and thought we'd drop by and say hi."

"Was she trying to catch with her left hand?" Morton asks.

Jonah nods. "She's good, too."

"She really is," Morton agrees. "Yesterday I saw her practicing, so I tried to throw my apple up and catch it with my left hand, but it landed on the grass."

"You could practice now," I say, thinking fast. "We'll head up to the princess's room. I'll bet if you work on catching for the next hour or so, you'll be great at it."

The guard tosses up the apple and sticks out his hand, but the apple lands on his foot. He frowns. "Maybe I will practice," he says. "Oh, wait, Princess Coco isn't back yet. She's probably still out riding."

He was clearly asleep when she came home *and* when she left again. "Could we wait in her room?" Jonah asks. "It's so hot out."

Morton wipes his forehead. "Sure is." He glances around, then looks back at us. "Yeah, you kids go up. Highest floor, second door on the left. If it's not pink, it's not Coco's."

This is one helpful guard.

"Thanks," I tell him.

Morton walks us to the front of the castle and nods at the soldier standing there. The soldier steps aside.

I love when things work out.

With Frederic on Jonah's shoulder, and Prince trotting behind us, we walk right into the empty castle. It's wonderfully cool inside. Since my flip-flops are pretty muddy at this point, I take them off and motion for Jonah to wipe his feet before going any farther. Ahhh. The polished bamboo floor feels great against my bare feet.

"What if Coco comes home early and catches us in her room?" Jonah asks worriedly as we dash up the winding staircase.

"One of us should keep watch out the window," I say, running with my flip-flops in hand. Prince pads behind me and Frederic clings to Jonah's shoulder. "If we see her riding up, we'll quickly get out of her room and hide till the coast is clear, then make our way out of the castle," I say.

"Or," Jonah adds, panting, "if she sees us in her room, she might get freaked out and throw Frederic against the wall. Which could change him back."

There's no telling what that mean princess will do if she catches the frog in her bedroom. If she doesn't like adorable furry dogs with floppy ears, why would she like a frog with bulging eyes? No matter how cute Frederic is in his little shorts.

We stop at a landing. No one is around. We go up another flight of winding stairs. Then another.

Finally, we come to the top floor. We hurry to the second door on the left. I open the door. Pink has exploded in this room.

"Wow," Jonah says. "Princess Coco's room is definitely pink. And look at all the things she has in here! There are a million stuffed animals! And toys! And ribbons!"

Frederic hops through the door and takes a flying leap onto the pink dresser. He suctions himself to one of the drawers. "Can someone help me open this?" he asks.

"Why?" I wonder aloud.

Frederic stares at me. "I want to change the pillowcase, of course," he says. "I don't think the princess would appreciate a slimy frog on her pillow. As a royal myself, I know I wouldn't."

Jonah opens the drawer and Frederic peers inside.

The frog's eyes widen. "Oh, wow!" Frederic says. "This is where she keeps her tiaras! Look at all the rubies and diamonds!"

I shut the drawer and glare at Jonah. "We should not be snooping."

Frederic hops off. "I suppose you're right," he says.

Suddenly, there are heavy footsteps on the stairs. Uh-oh. Someone is headed this way!

Maybe Princess Coco forgot something and came back! Or maybe the guards realized we're imposters and are going to arrest us!

"Everyone hide!" I order as I pull my brother, our dog, and Frederic with me into the best hiding spot I can find.

* chapter eleven *

Step Away From the Diary

"Hey, where did they go?" a deep voice asks.

They — meaning Jonah, Prince, Frederic, and I — are wedged in the back of Princess Coco's closet, behind a few big leather satchels full of arrows. Sparkly shoes line the floor and pretty tulle-skirted dresses hang from hooks. We are all silent, even Prince. My heart is racing.

"Huh," the same voice says. "I thought they were waiting in here." We hear something drop on the ground. "Why am I so bad at this?"

I glance at Jonah, and then I peer through the keyhole of the closet door.

It's the round, bald guard — Morton. The apple, now a mostly eaten core, is on the floor. The guard picks it up, throws it in the air, and tries — and fails — to catch it with his left hand.

"It's safe," I whisper to everyone.

Jonah nods. I open the door, and we all fall out of the closet.

"Oh, there you are," Morton says. He's holding a stack of clothing in his free hand. "No offense, but I brought you some clean clothes to change into. Yours were a little, um, smelly."

I nod understandingly. They certainly are. And I blame Princess Coco for leaving me in the well.

"They're Princess Coco's old T-shirts and shorts," Morton explains, placing the clothes on the bed, "but they're in good condition. We've been meaning to donate them to charity."

"Thank you!" I tell him. "We appreciate it!"

Morton nods. "Also, you should know that the soldier at the door informed me that Princess Coco left for the night. She's spending the evening at her eldest sister's boarding school an hour away from here," he explains. "She'll be back early in the morning. Did you come from far to see her?"

"You have no idea," I say.

"Well, you're welcome to stay the night since you're friends of the princess. She won't mind."

"She won't?" I ask in disbelief.

Morton shrugs. "Her bark is worse than her bite."

Ruff! Prince barks. His bark is worse than his bite, too. Not that he's ever bitten anyone.

I hope he doesn't bite anyone.

I also hope he doesn't pee on the princess's carpet or munch on her royal shoe collection.

"If you need anything, just ask for Morton. That's me," Morton says. "Oh, and Reginald might come by, too."

Since I'm supposed to be friends with Coco, I should probably know who Reginald is.

A bell rings. A loud, shrill bell. Then it rings again.

"I have to go," he says. "That's the king calling. Can't keep the king waiting, you know." He walks to the door. "You'll find extra blankets in the closet. Bye now!"

I glance at my watch. It's only two thirty at home. I spot an alarm clock on the nightstand beside the princess's bed. It says seven thirty P.M. I watch the two clocks and wait for them to change. 7:31. 7:32. When the princess's clock changes to 7:33, my watch changes to 2:31. That means that time *is* moving three times as fast here as it is at home.

So if we want to get home by seven A.M. wake-up, we have

to leave by nine A.M. here. But really more like eight thirty if we want to get back in our beds before our parents come into our rooms.

We have thirteen hours left in this fairy tale.

That's tons of time!

I look at the clothes Morton left on Coco's bed. Shorts and T-shirts. I hand Jonah the smaller set, a white T-shirt and blue shorts. I'll wear the purple T-shirt and denim shorts.

Jonah goes into the closet to change, and then I do.

Ahh. Fresh, clean clothes have never felt so good! I drop our dirty pajamas in the corner of the closet and make a mental note to remember to take them home. I am often forgetting pajamas in fairy tales.

When I come back into the room, Jonah is checking out Coco's toys. And boy, does she have a ton of toys. She has puzzles. She has LEGOs. She has stuffed animals piled in a corner. She has a princess castle.

Ha! Princesses have princess castles!

There's a canopy bed. Of course there is. There always is in princess rooms. It must be in the princess manual.

On the wall across from the bed is a painted mural. I step a bit closer to make out what it is.

It's the palace we're in, with a braided rainbow above it. Surrounding the palace are lush giant trees and purple and orange flowers. It's beautiful. It looks like it was made by a professional artist.

On another wall is a very small bureau with a round mirror. I laugh at my reflection. Apparently a trip down a waterfall makes for very messy hair.

I wonder if this mirror is our portal home? We never know what our portal home is going to be. It's sometimes a mirror but not always. I knock on it quickly to see if anything happens.

Nothing. Guess it's not the mirror. Although mirrors sometimes only work when they're ready.

Across from the bureau is a small desk with a stack of pink books on it and two tall candlesticks. A chair with a padded pink cushion is pushed under the desk. There's a small, plush pink chaise under the window. In one corner is a bow. Not a hair bow — an archery bow. I guess the one that goes with all the arrows in the closet. In another corner is a rocking horse. The pink carpet under my bare feet is soft, but looks well worn.

There is something off about the room. But what?

First of all, it's very pink. So pink. I have nothing against pink, but I feel like I'm drowning in cotton candy.

It's something else, though.

What is it?

I picture Coco in my mind. Choppy, short blond hair and the tiara was all I could see from my position at the bottom of the well. I have no idea how old she is. How tall she is. But I did have an entire not-so-nice conversation with her. She didn't sound like a kid Jonah's age. Or even my age.

"Did you guys get a good look at Coco?" I ask Jonah and Frederic.

Jonah picks up a stuffed pink dragon. "Kind of," he says.

"Yes," says Frederic. "I've followed her around all day, as you'll recall."

"How old is she?" I ask.

"Fourteen or fifteen," Frederic says. "A year or two younger than me."

I stifle a laugh. I never think of frogs as having an age. Then again, Frederic probably means his human age.

I pick up one of the stuffed animals. A sea lion wearing a sparkly pink T-shirt. "Doesn't this room seem young?" I ask

Frederic and Jonah. "Like it's for a kid and not a teenager? Are we sure this is Coco's room? Maybe she has a younger sister."

"Cassandra's the youngest. And" — Frederic points to the window — "it has her nickname on it. No one would use a royal's nickname. That would be treason."

"Morton would have told us if we had the wrong room," Jonah says.

"Good point. But it looks like a little kid's room. Strange."

"Maybe she just really likes stuffed animals," Jonah says. "And bows and arrows."

Frederic leaps up onto the canopy bed. "I don't really care about the décor," he says. "Can we focus on me? Maybe you can throw me against the wall here and see if that works?" He nods at Jonah.

"Or you could try the pillow version first," I reply. "Less painful."

"But you said the original version of the story involves a wall," Frederic reminds me. "With me landing against it. So let's begin by attempting that."

"No problem," Jonah says. He picks up Frederic and looks around at the different walls.

"Don't use the rainbow one," I tell him, gesturing to the mural. "It looks hand-painted."

"Yeah, I don't want to get frog guts on it," Jonah says.

"I definitely don't think the princess would appreciate frog guts on her mural," I say.

Frederic gulps. "No frog guts on *any* of the walls, please," he adds.

Poor Frederic. It has to be scary getting thrown at walls. "Jonah will be careful," I assure him.

"Got it. No frog guts," Jonah says. He winds up his arm, aims at the wall behind the bed, and fires.

I hold my breath.

Whoosh —

Smack!

"Still a frog?" Frederic asks, lying with his back on the carpet and his little green legs in the air.

"Still a frog," I say with a sigh. I bend down to help him up, and I pat him on the head.

Frederic rubs the back of his neck. "That hurt."

"Why don't you try the pillow now?" I ask. "Here, let me help you." He climbs onto the palm of my hand, and I lower him onto the center of the pink lace pillowcase. I guess we can put on fresh linens after we're done.

"What now?" Frederic asks, crossing his legs. "Should I attempt to take a nap?"

"Absolutely," I say. "That's what happens in one of the versions of the story. You fall asleep and then you turn into a prince."

"I'll try," he says, and closes his eyes.

I watch him.

He opens his eyes. "Stop staring at me."

"Sorry," I say. "I'll do something else."

He closes his eyes again and I wander around the room. Prince is busy batting around a pink stuffed kitten.

"Wow, the princess is writing a book," Jonah says, standing in front of Coco's desk.

I glance over. A notebook is lying open next to one of the candlesticks. On the other side of the desk, there's an entire stack of pink notebooks with a pencil lying across the cover of the one on top. She must really like to write stories.

"She has good handwriting," Jonah says, looking at the open notebook. "Every *i* is dotted and the *g*'s and *p*'s have perfect swirls."

I wish I had good handwriting. When I'm filling in Mad Libs, Robin and Frankie always have to ask me what something I wrote actually says.

Jonah starts reading.

" 'Today, when I was playing ball, I dropped it into the well,' " Jonah begins to read out loud. " 'There was a girl stuck in there and she asked me to help her. Maybe I should have. But I didn't feel like having a whole conversation with her. I wouldn't even know what to say. Does that make me a terrible person? Probably. I know you would have helped her. You always helped everyone. I banged my elbow on my desk this morning and started to cry, not because it hurt that bad but because you always hugged me any time I had the tiniest injury. I miss you so much, Mom.' "

Oh my gosh. I realize what Jonah has read. My heart pinches. It's something very private. Jonah opens his mouth to keep on reading, but I cut him off.

"STOP READING!" I yell.

"Huh? Why? It's a good story," Jonah says.

"It's a TRUE story," I tell him. "It's Coco's diary!"

"Oops," Jonah says, dropping the journal like a hot potato. "I didn't know!" He picks up the pencil from the top book on the stack and looks at the front cover. "Double oops," he adds.

DIARY is written in gold on the front of the book.

Yikes. I read someone's diary. Well, someone read me someone's diary.

A princess's diary. A princess who already hates me.

But what I heard makes me feel really bad for Princess Coco.

She misses her mom. She writes her diary entries to her mom.

Is her mom dead?

Poor Coco.

I wish I hadn't read — well, listened to — her diary. What an invasion of Coco's privacy! I didn't mean to do it, but still. I sit on the bed with a funny feeling in my chest.

"Sad, huh," Jonah says.

I nod. "Diaries are private," I remind him. "I'm going to forget I ever read that. And so should you!"

"Forgotten," he says. Then he gets that strange look on his face. "Hey, I'm trying to forget Coco's diary, but I just remembered something *else.* Someone once read Maryrose's diary!"

Really? "Who?" I ask.

Jonah starts scratching his head. "Jax!" he says. "It was her cousin Jax. She was so mad at him she wouldn't speak to him for a week!"

"Oh," I say. I could totally see Jax reading someone's diary — on purpose. Jonah and I did it by accident, at least.

I glance back at Frederic on the bed. His little froggy chest is rising and falling. He seems to be asleep.

He's asleep! I mouth to Jonah, excited. This is it! Frederic will sleep, and then wake up, and then he'll be transformed. Then we can go home and Princess Coco will never know that we were in her room and accidentally read her diary.

Prince spots a stuffed animal that looks a lot like Snoopy, and he woofs hello.

"*Shh*," Jonah says. "Frederic's sleeping."

Frederic's eyes pop open. "Of course I'm not sleeping! How could anyone sleep with the three of you around? Have you ever heard of indoor voices?"

Crumbs.

"Hey," booms an unfamiliar boy's voice at the door. "Let's go have some fun!"

* chapter twelve *

Friends

Standing in the doorway, hands on his hips, is a teenaged boy around Princess Coco's — and I guess Frederic's — age. His dark brown hair is slicked back, and he's wearing a gray T-shirt and billowy green pants with black sandals. His toenails are painted a sparkly dark blue. Cool. Maybe I can find that shade when we get back to Smithville.

"Who are you two?" the guy asks, looking from me to Jonah.

"Morton — the guard — let us up here," I explain. "We're Coco's friends. We were invited to stay until Coco gets back tomorrow morning from visiting her sister." I take a step to the left to shield Frederic from the boy's view. He would probably think it was very strange that a frog was in here. Though I guess I could say Frederic is our pet. Although he'd probably find that even stranger.

"Gotcha," the guy says, walking over to the mirror above Coco's dresser and running his hands through his hair. "The tropical humidity in Birdopolis is a killer on frizz," he adds.

So Birdopolis *is* the name of this kingdom. It definitely fits.

"Are you a friend of Princess Coco's?" Jonah asks the boy.

"A friend? Try her *best* friend," he says. "I'm Reginald. I forgot Coco was going to her sister's recital tonight. Her dad used to do all that stuff, but now he can't."

I think about what Coco wrote in her diary about her mom. "Why not?" I ask.

"The king — her dad — is really sick," Reginald says. "I feel so bad about that . . . especially because her mom died. But now her dad isn't well enough to go to school events for her sisters, so Coco does that."

Aww. Princess Coco doesn't have such an easy life. And it sounds like she's kind of nice. But how can she be nice when she's proven herself to be EVIL?

Maybe she's only nice to her relatives. And her best friend.

"Ooh, is that a puppy?" Reginald asks, walking over to

Prince, who is still nosing through a pile of Coco's stuffed animals. "You're so stinkin' cute!" he adds, giving Prince a good scratch under his chin.

Ruff! Prince barks appreciatively.

"Are you guys enjoying Coco's room?" Reginald asks, straightening up. He looks around and frowns. "Don't get me wrong — I looove Coco. But this room — it's for a six-year-old. My little brother and sister would be in heaven here, but it's no fun for a teenager."

"True," I say, glad that I'm not the only one who noticed.

Reginald looks like he's about to say something else, but then he shrugs and says, "I'm kind of bored without Coco around. Do you guys want to go swimming? There are always extra bathing suits by the pool."

"Yay, swimming!" Jonah cries.

Prince wags his tail and lets out an excited yelp.

"Jonah, we're kind of in the middle of something," I say between my teeth, motioning to Frederic with my chin, hoping Reginald won't spot him.

"We're going swimming is what we're doing," Frederic says, jumping onto his webbed feet. "Swimming always tires me out, and I'm having trouble falling asleep."

Reginald squints at Frederic. "Um, you guys? You have a talking frog." He glances at me and Jonah in confusion. "Did you know that?"

"Yup!" Jonah says. "Don't try and eat him, 'kay?"

"I won't," Reginald says, cocking his head to the side. "But I did eat frog legs once. They tasted like chicken."

"So I've heard," Frederic grumbles as he hops off the bed.

I scoop up Prince, and Reginald leads the way down the four flights of stairs to the front door. It's still hot outside, but the sun isn't as intense as earlier. I look at my watch. I hope we have time for this.

As we step onto the patio, a giant yellow bird with a long black beak swoops past my head on its way to a palm tree.

"Monkey!" Jonah says, pointing at a little brown monkey swinging from a vine.

"You guys are definitely not from around here," Reginald says as we walk toward the pool. "You'll find a chest of bathing suits in the shed," he adds, pointing to a white wooden hut. "I'm already wearing my suit under my pants."

In minutes, Jonah and I are changed into bathing suits. Even Frederic has found floral swimming trunks that were probably made for a toy but look just about right for him.

The pool is huge, with sparkling blue water and lots of cool pool stuff, like floaties and noodles, just as Frederic said. The guard he saw earlier is gone.

"Geronimo!" Frederic yells, and cannonballs into the pool.

Reginald dives in next, followed by Jonah and even Prince.

I jump in and swim around. The water is cool and calm. This is so much better than well water. Not to mention the scary waterfall.

"Thanks for inviting us to swim," I tell Reginald, who's balancing on a blue floatie. His eyes are closed and his hands are crossed behind his head.

"No problem. Any friends of Coco's are friends of mine," he says.

Gulp. Should I tell him we're not really friends of Princess Coco's?

Splash! Jonah did another cannonball. Water sprays on all of us.

"Careful, Jonah!" Frederic yells. "You almost drowned me!"

But I can't help but splash Jonah back. And then Reginald splashes me. The three of us get into a huge splash fight, laughing while Prince cheers us on with barks.

The more fun we have, the guiltier I feel about not telling Reginald the truth. But if we tell him the truth, he'll probably make us leave. And we can't leave until Frederic has slept on the princess's pillow!

"Want to know a secret?" Reginald asks us when we're done with our water fight.

I swim over to his float. Jonah pops up from under the water.

"I know you guys aren't Coco's friends," Reginald says.

I look at Jonah. Crumbs. What will Reginald do? Call the guards? We'll be in big trouble.

"How did you know?" Jonah asks, squinting up at Reginald in the sunshine.

Reginald chuckles. "I know because Princess Coco only has one friend — me."

"Oh," I say, thinking about how lucky I am to have Frankie and Robin as my best friends. I wonder if Princess Coco is lonely.

"So who *are* you guys, then?" Reginald asks, glancing from me to Jonah.

"We're Abby and Jonah." I motion to myself and my brother. "And Prince." I nod at our dog. "And Frederic the talking frog."

I decide I might as well be honest. "We're trying to help him turn human again."

"I am a prince," Frederic says while doing the doggie — froggy? — paddle. He shoots a haughty look at Prince. "A *real* prince."

"Oh," Reginald says, looking surprised. "Seriously?"

I nod. "Where I come from," I explain, "there's a famous story about a princess who throws a frog against a wall and turns him human again. We were trying to see if that would work here."

"You want Coco to throw him against a wall?" Reginald asks, pointing to Frederic, in shock.

"No," I say, treading water. "Well, maybe. We're going to try some other stuff first. Like having Frederic sleep on her pillow."

Reginald laughs. "She's not going to like that at all. But don't worry. I won't tell her."

"Thank you," I say gratefully. "We don't want her to hate us. She's kind of scary."

Reginald sighs and flips off the float into the water. "I hear ya. Sometimes she's tough to get to know. But once she opens up, she's really sweet."

If he says so.

"Well, the sun's going down so I have to get home," Reginald tells us. He swims to the side of the pool, hops out, and grabs a towel. Then he disappears into the shed and comes out a minute later, dressed. He slicks back his hair. "Bye, you guys. If you're hungry, there are probably chicken fingers in the fridge. Help yourself. I always do."

"Yum," Jonah says.

I realize I'm hungry. Jonah and I each do one last cannonball, and then we climb out of the pool with Frederic and Prince, dry off, and change. Back inside the castle, we look for the kitchen.

"Can I help you?" asks a tiny woman dressed all in white.

The four of us freeze.

"Um, we're friends of Coco's," I say. "We're looking for the kitchen."

"Right that way," she says, pointing us down the hall. "Enjoy."

I have to say, the security is a little too relaxed around here. It's a good thing we're not a band of robbers.

In case you're wondering, bands of robbers are real things. I met them in another fairy tale.

We find our way to the marble kitchen, open the fancy silver fridge, and serve ourselves a heaping plate of coleslaw and chicken fingers.

"Mmm," I say.

Prince makes sloppy eating sounds.

"Delicious," says Jonah. He smiles at Frederic. "Tastes just like frog legs."

I laugh so hard I snort coleslaw out of my nose.

Frederic sticks his tongue out us.

When we're done, we sneak back up the stairs, tired and full. The castle is so quiet. I wonder if it's always like this. No hustle, no bustle. No one around.

The clock says 10:00 P.M. and my watch says it's 3:20 A.M. at home.

As we step into Coco's room, I yawn. "So we continue with the plan. Frederic, do you think you can fall asleep now?"

He yawns, too. "I think so."

"Good. Hopefully, when you wake up, you'll be a prince again."

"I'd better be," Frederic says. He hops on the bed and folds himself onto one of the pillows in a little heap.

We wait. And watch.

I motion to Jonah to be quiet.

Prince climbs onto the daybed and buries his head under a front leg.

We stare at Frederic.

His breathing slows.

Eventually, we hear, "Snooooort!"

He's asleep! I mouth. Yay! I watch him a little longer. "But he's still a frog," I say with a sigh. "He didn't turn back." My eyes feel heavy.

"Maybe you have to fall asleep beside him," Jonah says.

"I can't do that. We don't have that much time left. If we sleep until morning, we'll be in trouble," I say, feeling increasingly tired. I guess playing in the pool wore me out. Jonah looks tired, too.

"Just sleep until midnight," Jonah says. "Magical things always happen at midnight, right?"

"Good point," I whisper back.

"You take a nap," he says. "I'll stay awake and keep watch."

My brother's eyes are half-closed.

"Maybe I should set her alarm just in case you fall asleep, too. For twelve-oh-five."

"Okay," Jonah says yawning. "Do that."

I reach over and set the alarm next to Coco's bed. I yawn again.

"Okay," I say. "Power nap."

My brother stretches out on the daybed beside Prince.

I stretch out on the second pillow next to a snoring Frederic.

Sleeeeeepy.

Sleeepy.

Sleee —

"AHHHHHHH! WHAT IS HAPPENING?" a voice screeches.

My eyes pop open. I was fast asleep.

Wait a minute. When we went to bed, it was dark. Now bright sunshine is streaming through the windows.

I glance at the clock next to Coco's bed.

It's not 12:05!

It's 6 A.M. I glance at my watch. It's 6 A.M. at home, too.

The alarm didn't go off . . . again! Why am I having such bad luck with alarms?

I sit up superfast.

Princess Coco is standing at the door!

Her face is flushed red, and her hands are on her hips as she glares at me. "What are you doing in my bed?"

* chapter thirteen *

There's Just Something About You

"I will get the soldiers and have you thrown into the dungeon! Soldiers! Soldiers!" Princess Coco shrieks.

I clamber off the bed. "Don't! Please!" I beg. We have no time for jail.

"Yeah, don't!" Jonah echoes, springing off the daybed, his hair all messed up.

Prince wakes up and starts barking. Somehow, Frederic is still able to sleep in the middle of all the chaos.

"GUARDS!" Princess Coco yells.

I brace myself for guards. Any second, they'll rush in and drag us off to the dungeon.

Except I don't hear any footsteps.

Coco starts tapping her foot.

Jonah and I stand frozen. Even Prince stops barking. We wait, and no one comes.

"The security here is not so great," Jonah says.

"No kidding," Coco says with a sigh. "It's the worst."

I think about her diary. And how quiet it is in the castle. "Is anyone else even here?" I ask.

"That's none of your business," she snaps.

"It kind of is," Jonah says. "We either have to make a run for it or we don't."

Coco rolls her eyes. "My dad doesn't have the best hearing, and my sisters are away at boarding school. The guards are probably still sleeping. And my mom . . ." She looks down at her hands. "My mom died. A long time ago. When I was little."

I swallow. Poor Coco. I glance around the room again. Stuffed animals. Toys. Pink galore. Suddenly, I wonder if Coco has kept it this way because her mom had decorated it for her, when Coco was little.

I take a cautious step toward the princess. "Please don't call anyone else," I say again. "We're not here to hurt you in any way."

She snorts. "As if *you* two could hurt me. I'm tough." She lifts up her right arm and makes a muscle. "Two kids and some floppy-eared mutt don't scare me."

"Two kids, a floppy-eared mutt, and a frog," Jonah clarifies.

"A what?" Coco asks, staring at Jonah.

"A frog," he says, and points to Frederic.

I think that might have been a case of TMI — too much information.

I look at Frederic, who is still very much a green frog. Boo. We slept the whole night and it didn't work! He's going to be *so* disappointed. I'm disappointed.

Coco finally notices the frog. Her eyes practically pop out. "You put a frog on my pillow?" she screams. "What is wrong with you people?"

"It's for a good reason!" I say. "He's not really a frog!"

"He sure looks like a frog," she fumes.

"He's really a prince. The Frog Prince," I explain quickly. "He was cursed into being a frog. But we thought that if he spent the night on your pillow, he might change back into a prince."

"Well, he didn't," Coco says. "So get him off!"

Her shout finally makes Frederic's eyes open. I see him reach his little green hand to his nose to double-check that he is, indeed, still a frog. His face crinkles in disappointment.

Princess Coco shakes her head and points to the door. "All of you — out!"

"Please, Princess Coco!" Frederic begs, hopping off the bed. "You have to help me! You must! I've been trying to get your attention for days." He hops over to her, his little green hands pressed together. "Surely you have a fairy or witch in your royal court who can change me back! You don't understand what I've been through. I used to be royal just like you! I slept in a bed. I was waited on hand and foot. I put on my tuxedo and danced at balls. I rode in a royal carriage. I had servants remove the crust from my sandwiches, feed me grapes, and fan me on hot days! I was normal!"

That's normal?

I glance at Coco. Frederic definitely has her attention now.

"Please help me," he begs. He gazes up at her.

Coco bites her lip. "There are no fairies or witches in Birdopolis," she says with a sigh. Her tone has softened and she sounds a little nicer. I remember what Reginald said about her. *Is Coco actually nice, under all that attitude?*

"You can help another way," I say quickly.

"How?" Coco asks suspiciously.

"Kiss me!" Frederic says.

She grimaces. "*Kiss* you? That's disgusting!"

"Please," Frederic begs. "I promise to reward you if I turn back to a human prince. I'll give you whatever you want from my kingdom. Anything. We'll get married!"

Coco looks shocked. "Why would you think I'd want to marry *you*?"

"You will when I turn back," he promises. "I'm quite handsome. But you don't have to marry me. Just name your price."

She raises an eyebrow. "Can I have your army?"

"My army?" he asks.

"Yes," she says. "I clearly need new security."

Frederic nods. "Fine. You can have my army." He hops back on the bed and stands on the pillow. "Now kiss me! Please!"

Princess Coco hesitates, but then follows Frederic back to the bed. She leans down. She puckers her lips and squishes her eyes closed.

She kisses him.

"Ew," Jonah says.

"Shush," I tell him.

We wait.

Nothing happens. Crumbs.

"It didn't work," Coco says softly. "I'm sorry."

"Wait," Jonah cries. "Try throwing him against the wall! It's fun."

"Yes!" I say. "Please try!" It has to work. It just has to.

"*Ooooookay,*" Princess Coco says with a shrug. "Like that's not weird or anything."

"Just do it," Frederic snaps. "Do you want my army or not?"

I'm surprised by his harsh tone, but I know we're all getting impatient here.

Princess Coco picks up the frog. She closes one eye, aims toward the wall behind her bed, and throws.

Splat!

Ruff! Prince barks.

Frederic hits the wall and slowly slides down, down, down behind the canopy bed.

"Did it work?" the princess asks. "Do I get his army?"

"No," croaks Frederic from behind the bed. "I'm still a stupid frog! Why didn't it work?"

"I don't know," I say. I'm starting to feel desperate. "That's what happened in the original story! The princess threw you!"

Frederic pops out from under the bed and stomp-hops angrily across the carpet. "That stupid fairy and her stupid curse ruined my life!"

Jonah starts scratching his head.

"Why did she curse you anyway?" Coco asks. "What did you do?"

Scratch, scratch, scratch.

"Nothing!" Frederic cries. He angrily pulls himself back on top of the mattress. "She did it JUST TO BE EVIL. She's a horrible big-chinned fairy freak!"

Now my brother is scratching with both hands. He has that funny look on his face again.

"Jonah, are you okay?" I ask.

My brother shakes his head. *"I did not do it to be evil!"* he yells. *"And I do not have a big chin!"*

We all look at Jonah.

"Huh?" I say.

"You?" says Frederic. "What are you talking about? You're not the fairy."

Jonah shakes his head again. He points at Frederic. "I'm not. But Maryrose is. I remember! She was the one that changed you into a frog!"

HUH?

Maryrose cursed Frederic?

But why?

If Maryrose changed him . . .

I turn to Frederic. "Why would Maryrose change you into a frog?" I demand.

"Because she's horrible!" Frederic squawks. "A horrible, evil fairy freak!"

Is she? Should I be worried about Maryrose? Should Jonah and I not trust her?

"No!" Jonah yells, still scratching his head like crazy. "He's lying! I remember! Yes, Maryrose was the one to turn him into a frog, but that was because Frederic was a mean and terrible prince! He used to steal things from his big sister all the time! Then his sister was made queen, and Frederic . . . Frederic tried to kill her!"

Coco and I gasp. Frederic is silent. Prince whimpers.

"Yes! He tried to kill his sister to get the throne!" Jonah adds, his eyes wide as he keeps on scratching.

Princess Coco takes a step back from Frederic in horror. "You should be arrested!" she cries, pointing at him.

"Is that true?" I ask Frederic.

"No, no, no!" Frederic yells. He thrashes at the pillow. Then he hops all over the bed. He is losing it. He's throwing a temper tantrum. "None of you know what you're talking about! Maryrose is a freak! And you, little boy," he screams at Jonah, "are a liar! A big fat liar! A big, fat, lying freak!"

"Don't talk about my brother like that!" I yell.

"I will talk about your brother any way I want!" he yells. "You, your stupid smelly dog, and your brother. Your brother that keeps scratching his head. He probably has lice! I can't believe I let you people *kiss* me! Disgusting!"

"My dog is not smelly and my brother does not have lice!" I shout. "He's remembering something!"

Frederic is hopping up and down like a maniac. A maniac frog. "You put your peasant, germy lips all over me! I could barely keep myself from vomiting!"

Wow. He's *mean*.

Frederic keeps jumping up and down on the bed as he screams at us. "You're all disgusting! But Jonah is the worst! He almost drowned me in the pool with all his splashing! He has a stuffed frog! And he likes to eat frog legs!"

"Stop talking about my brother!" I order.

"Why should I?" he yells as he jumps in my face. "Your brother is a dumb kid. The dumbest of the dumb!"

"No. One. Calls. My. Brother. Dumb!" I shout. Then I wave my hand to get Frederic away from me.

My hand connects with his little green body.

He goes flying toward the wall with the rainbow mural on it.

SMACK.

Oh wow. Oh my.

I really hope I'm not about to see frog guts.

Coco will definitely haul me off to the dungeon herself for that.

But no. I don't see frog guts.

Instead, the frog starts to stretch. And stretch. His face stretches, his arms stretch, his legs stretch. His skin color goes from green to bronze. His bald green head sprouts thick black hair.

His eyes stay the same. I wonder if they were always that bulgy.

He's wearing brown pants, a brown shirt, and a crown.

He's tall. Really tall. And wide. And strong. He towers over all of us.

He's a human again.

He's a prince.

A mean, scary prince.

* chapter fourteen *

I'll Take These

Hah!" Prince Frederic says, admiring himself in the mirror. "I'm back! I'm no longer a filthy frog. I'm human. I'm big. Huge! I'm glad I kept doing my push-ups. Look at these biceps! Now I can return to my kingdom. Now nothing will stop me!"

"*We* have to stop him!" Jonah cries. "Maryrose was the one that cursed him. She doesn't want him to be human!"

"You can't stop me from leaving," Frederic scoffs. He grabs a candlestick off the desk and threatens Jonah with it.

"Leave the boy alone!" Princess Coco yells.

"What do you care?" he says. "You didn't want these losers here anyway. Dump all three of them in your well and be done with them." He rushes over to Coco's dresser, opens the top drawer, and scoops up a tiara. "This is nice. I think I'll take it."

"Hey! You put that back!" Princess Coco shouts. "The tiaras were my mom's!"

"Now who has the power, huh? I've been hopping after you for days, hoping to plead my case to you," Frederic shouts at Coco. "But you never even looked my way. Or gave me the time of day. You're meaner than I am!"

"I am *not*," she says.

"Are so. Come with me! We'll form an alliance, take over my kingdom, and then take over yours! You don't even have an army! And your king is useless!"

"My father is sick," she snaps, her face reddening. "And I'm not going with you. My mother would not approve."

He snorts. "What do you care? She's dead!"

Jonah and I gasp.

Coco's face twists in pain. "Get out of here," she whispers. "Now."

"Fine," Frederic says with a shrug. "Stay here. Whatever. But I'm taking these." He grabs three more tiaras and starts looping them over his arm.

"You are not!" She stomps her foot. "Dog!" she yells. "Attack! Attack!"

Dog? Is she talking to Prince?

Prince seems to think so. He starts barking like crazy and snapping at Frederic's leg.

Without even blinking, Frederic conks Prince on the head with the candlestick.

OH, NO!

Princess Coco gasps.

"Prince!" I holler.

Jonah bends down to comfort him. Prince's eyes are closed.

"Is he breathing?" I ask, my heart pounding. I kneel down to examine Prince. I'm going to cry. "Let me help him!"

"There are four of us and only one of you!" Jonah tells Frederic, standing up and puffing out his chest. "You won't get away with this! Coco! Get your bow and arrows! Stop him!"

"Me?" she says, surprised. "I'm not a soldier."

"She's not going to stop me!" Frederic laughs. "She's just a pathetic princess!"

"Guards! Guards!" the princess yells.

"*I'll* stop him, then!" yells Jonah. He runs toward the closet to get the arrows. Frederic slams the door on him and locks him inside.

"Jonah!" I cry. Thankfully, Prince's eyes open then. He looks a little shell-shocked, but he's fine. He shakily gets to his feet and lets out a bark.

"I'm out of here," Frederic says and takes off.

Prince goes running after him.

"Prince!" I yell. "Come back! He's dangerous!" Princess Coco is just standing in the middle of her room, frozen. And Jonah is stuck inside the closet. At least he's safe in there, for now.

I race out the door. Frederic is running down the hallway with Prince close behind. Why isn't there anyone around? Doesn't anyone care that he's about to steal Coco's tiaras and jewels?

"Thief! Thief!" I cry as Frederic races down the stairs. "Someone help! Stop that man!"

But no one comes.

Frederic throws a tiara at my head and I duck. "These don't even have diamonds on them!" he wails. "Cheap garbage." He keeps throwing tiaras at me, and one scrapes across my arm. Ouch.

I run as fast as I can. I get to the first floor of the palace just in time to see Frederic burst through the palace doors. The scrawny soldier is still guarding it.

Yes! He'll stop Frederic!

"Stop!" the soldier yells. He rushes toward Frederic.

But Frederic just pushes him out of the way with his arm. The guard is out cold!

Frederic runs right toward the palace wall. Maybe Morton is there, in his chair? Hopefully, he's not asleep. Maybe he'll stop Frederic!

I rush through the archway. Morton IS back in his chair, but he's sleeping again!

Seriously?

I'm about to scream to wake him up, when Frederic stops short.

"Ah, he never fails me," Frederic suddenly says, looking straight ahead.

Huh? Who is he talking about?

That's when I see the carriage outside the palace wall. It's the fancy black one we saw earlier. Maybe someone is here to help us!

The driver jumps out of the carriage. Yes! He's going to help me!

I expect the driver to come running over, but instead he salutes Frederic. "Your Highness!" he says. "I watched you transform through the window! I've been waiting per your instructions!"

Oh, no. My stomach sinks. The driver is NOT going to help me.

"Greetings, loyal servant, Heinrich," Frederic says.

I scowl at Heinrich. He's tall and skinny and . . . wearing a blue hat! He must be who Jonah saw behind the tree right before he threw Frederick against it. And didn't Frederic hop over to check out if anyone was there? And didn't Frederic report back that there was only a tall plant with a *blue* flower?

What a liar! Obviously, Heinrich has been following Frederic around all day just waiting for him to be turned human again.

"Greetings, sir," Heinrich replies with a bow. "I've come to pick you up."

"Put this girl in the carriage," Frederic orders, motioning to me. "I've decided to keep her as my prisoner."

What? "You can't!" I cry, turning to run away. But Frederic grabs my arm.

Meanwhile, Morton continues to snooze.

"Oh, but I can," Frederic says. "You know Maryrose. I will keep you locked up just in case she tries something again."

"No!" I yell, struggling to get away, kicking at Prince Frederic.

"We'll imprison her in the dungeon as soon as we get home," Frederic tells his servant.

Ahhh! I can't get in the carriage! Jonah won't be able to save me on his own and Coco will never come after me to help. She left me in a well! She's not going to chase me to another kingdom. If I get in the carriage, I'll never get home.

I look around, desperate to run.

Prince is jumping up on Frederic, barking and barking, but Frederic just ignores him. And Prince still looks too weakened from his bump on the head to do much more than bark and jump.

Heinrich takes my other arm and together he and Frederic push me inside the carriage.

"What is her name again?" Heinrich asks Frederic.

Frederic laughs. "Crabby."

"Stay inside, Crabby," Heinrich tells me.

"It's Abby," I grumble as he slams the carriage door shut.

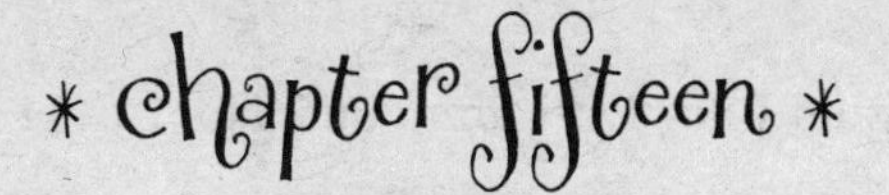

chapter fifteen

Giddyup

The carriage bounces down the road.

It's cramped in here and the seat is rubber and not that comfortable. Frederic is admiring himself in the reflection of the window as I glare at him.

I glance at my watch. It's 6:20 at home.

My parents' alarm goes off at 6:45. They come into my room at 7:00. I don't have much time!

The carriage is moving faster and faster. I have no idea where I'm going.

Yes, I do. To a dungeon in Frederic's kingdom. I feel sick. I have to get out of this carriage. I have to!

What should I do? Do I jump out? No. I can't. We're going way too fast.

Plus how could I run? I'm not even wearing my flip-flops!

I have to try and make a break for it. If I don't escape now, I'll never get home.

Heinrich, the driver, is sitting up front. Frederic is sitting beside me, still staring out the window. He's not even paying attention to me. He probably figures I won't try to escape a moving carriage.

Escape, I tell myself! Now is your chance!

I eye the handle.

All I have to do is pull on it and jump. On the count of three. One. Two. Three.

I don't move.

Okay, really this time.

One. Two. THREE.

I take a deep breath, grab the handle, push it open, and JUMP, all in one swoop.

I land on the ground on my knees. Ouch! That hurt. I think I skinned them. But they are still working.

"Stop the carriage!" I hear Frederic yell. But I don't wait for the carriage to stop. I run toward the forest.

"Come back!" I hear. "Crabby, come back!"

He's running after me. I have to hide. What do I do? Where do I go?

I look up at the trees. Can I climb up one of them and hide in the leaves? Yes! If Jonah did it; so can I!

I leap onto it.

I slide back down.

I can't. Jonah is the Spider-Man, not me. This tree is way too big for me to climb. I guess I can hide behind it.

"Okay, fine, I'll call you Abby!" Frederic shouts. He's getting closer! "Just come back! You're my prisoner!"

No! No, no, no! I have to hide.

I hear Frederic walking toward me and leap toward another tree and hide behind that one.

Wait. This place looks familiar. Have I been here before? Yes! I have.

There's my well! Well, not my well. But *the* well.

Frederic appears in front of me. "There you are," he says, his bulgy eyes looking mean. "Come on, Abby. Back to the carriage."

"No!" I yell. And with that, I run and leap into the well.

Splat. The drop is longer than I thought. The water burns my scraped knees and tiara-scratched arm.

But I'm safe. I'm safe! He can't get me out. He'll have to leave without me! I plaster myself against the side of the well. Maybe he won't see me.

His face appears at the top of the well. "I'm not leaving you in Birdopolis! You're coming with me!" he insists. "Don't you see? I have to keep you locked up. You're my special lucky charm against the evil Maryrose. If SHE tries to change me back into a frog, you can change me back to a prince again. You're the only one who was able to. You must be magical!"

"Maryrose isn't evil!" I yell up. "And I'm not magical!"

He rolls his eyes. "She turned me into a frog. And you turned me back. So she is, and you are."

"She only did that because you tried to kill your sister!" I shout up.

"It was none of her business. She wasn't even from Frogville! Just because my parents made her my sister's fairy godmother does not give her the right to turn me into a frog. Now I will go back and take you as my prisoner!"

"Isn't that what you said your *sister* did? Imprison ten-year-olds?" I snap.

Frederic laughs again. "I did say that, didn't I? I lied!

Ha! That's what *I* would do. Now come on. I don't have time for this. You must obey me. I am a royal and you're a nothing. I order you to get out of that well and to follow me back to the carriage."

"I'm not going with you!" I yell.

"Fine," Frederic grunts. "Stay here. Wither in this well. I have to get going. I have a kingdom to overtake." I hear him walking away.

I shiver. He's going to kill his sister.

Maryrose's goddaughter.

Mayrose would want me to help.

I freeze. Did Maryrose send us into this fairy tale to help her goddaughter?

To stop the prince from doing something awful?

My mind spins.

What do I know for sure?

I know that Maryrose turned Frederic into a frog to protect Sophie, his sister.

Then, according to the original Grimm story, the princess threw the frog against the wall and turned him back into a prince. Then they both returned to his kingdom.

It's supposed to be a happy ending.

But what if it isn't a happy ending? What if after the "happy ending," the prince kills his sister to take over the kingdom?

I gasp.

What if Maryrose sent me and Jonah here to *stop* Frederic from turning back into a prince?

Maryrose wanted him to stay a frog!

And at first her plan worked. We interrupted the story. We stopped the frog from catching the princess's ball. But then I threw him against a wall and changed him anyway. And now he's going to kill Sophie after all.

Oh, no! I have to fix this. I have to stop Frederic.

And I can't do that from the well.

"WAIT!" I yell up. "Frederic! Come back! I don't want to be stuck here! It's smelly! Help me out and I'll come with you!"

I hear his footsteps head back toward the well. He leans his head over the edge. "What do you want?"

"To come out. Pass me a branch. You'll probably find one right by the side of the well. Frogville doesn't sound so bad. Maybe I'll like it."

Frederic lowers down the same branch Jonah used earlier.

Once again I climb up.

At least I'll never have to be in that well again. It's disgusting.

"Hurry up," Frederic snaps when I step over the edge. "No more funny business. We're going back to Frogville."

I nod.

What else can I do?

* chapter sixteen *

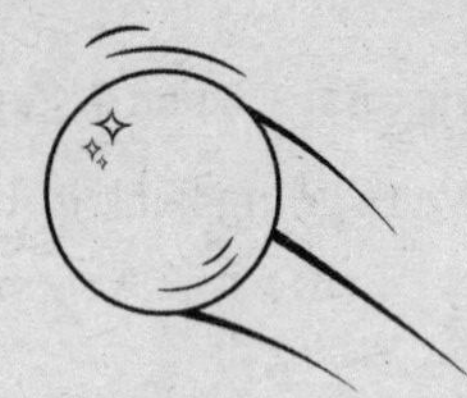

Commander Coco

When we reach the carriage, Frederic opens the door.

"Get in," he orders.

I hop in and he climbs in after me.

He wrinkles up his face. "You smell like a well."

"So do you," I remind him.

He sneers at me. "Step on it, Heinrich!" he orders.

The driver turns around. Except it isn't Heinrich.

It's Coco.

She's wearing Heinrich's blue hat. "Going somewhere?" she asks.

Frederic jumps and clutches his chest. "What are you doing here? Where's Heinrich?"

"He's otherwise occupied," Coco replies sharply. "And you are under arrest."

Go, Coco!

"Ha!" Frederic jeers. "You're putting me under arrest? You and what army?"

Coco smiles with her mouth closed. "Me and *my* army. The royal army. Which includes some furry friends."

Huh? Furry friends?

Frederic looks nervous. "I don't think so," he says, and opens his door to escape.

But when he does, Morton and two monkeys pounce on him. I laugh. The monkeys! They *are* loyal, just like Jonah said. And now they're part of Coco's army.

I spot Jonah and prince sitting high on top of a horse. I give my brother a thumbs-up.

Reginald is standing beside them, slicking back his hair.

"I showed up at the palace just as you pulled away," Reginald tells me. "Your little dog was barking like crazy. I followed him to Coco's room and found all the tiaras along the way —"

"I was standing there in shock," Coco says. "Reginald yelled at me that we had to help you, and of course he was right. I unlocked the closet and freed your brother and grabbed my bow and arrows and jumped on my horse." She turns to her friend. "Thank you for helping me do the right thing."

Ruff, ruff! Prince barks.

Jonah gives me a cheerful wave. I'm so relieved they're safe!

"Throw Frederic in the dungeon!" Coco orders. "And his henchman, too."

The soldiers grab Frederic and handcuff him. I see that Heinrich is already handcuffed and sitting sullenly on the side of the road.

Hurrah! I'm free!

I jump out of the carriage just as Jonah jumps off the horse. We give each other a big hug.

"You're okay!" Jonah says. "I was so worried!"

"I'm fine," I say. "Are you okay?"

Jonah nods. "Hey, were you in the well again?" he asks, sniffing the air.

"Don't ask," I sigh.

"Coco rounded up the soldiers and led them all down to the road to find you!" Jonah explains. "It was a good thing you stalled Frederic and got out of the carriage, or we never would have reached you in time. Did you see? I got the monkeys to come, too. Wasn't that smart of me?"

I nod. "I can't believe Coco helped me," I say. "I didn't think she would."

Coco steps out of the driver's seat in the carriage. "I couldn't bear to let Jonah lose you. I know how hard it is to lose someone you love."

"Told you she was nice," Reginald says, giving Coco a hip bump.

Huh. Maybe sometimes mean people can be nice deep down.

I look at Frederic, who is now tied around one of the massive trees.

And sometimes people you think are nice are actually mean deep down.

I guess you never know until you dig deep down.

I turn to Coco. "Thank you for helping us," I say. "I know you didn't have to."

"Someone has to protect my kingdom," she responds. "My father can't do it anymore. He's too old and sick. My eldest sister is going to be queen. So I guess it's up to me. I'm an excellent rider. I think fast. I have great aim. Once I master my left-hand skills I'll be unstoppable. Did you hear that, everyone?" Coco announces. "I'm becoming commander in chief!"

The soldiers, and the monkeys, all salute her.

Reginald high-fives her. "Awesome!" he says.

Ruff, Prince barks. Coco laughs and then actually bends down and gives Prince a scratch behind his ears.

"So what happens now?" Jonah asks me.

"We go home," I say.

Coco looks at Jonah and me. She looks a little sad. "You sure you don't want to stay longer? I'll let you play with the golden ball." She blushes.

Prince barks and wags his tail.

"Sure, *now* you'll let us," I say.

"I do want to play with that ball!" Jonah adds. "It looks really bouncy."

"It is," she says. "I can also show you how to shoot an arrow."

Jonah's face lights up. "I've always wanted to shoot an arrow!"

"We have to get home, Jonah," I point out. My watch says it's six thirty, which means we only have an hour and a half. My heart starts to race.

We never know what the portal to take us home is until we knock on it and it starts to swirl.

"We have to find something magical. Or someone magical." I turn to Coco. "Are you sure there aren't any fairies in your kingdom?"

She shakes her head. "Not that I know of."

"Something has to be magical around here," I say, trying to think.

"The well!" Jonah says.

I sigh. I guess I will have to go back inside the well after all.

Third time's a charm?

It's still smelly in the well.

Not that Prince seems to mind. He's barking and splashing all over the place.

"Good-bye!" Princess Coco calls to me and Jonah, leaning over the rim of the well with Reginald. "Take care!"

"You too!" I call out.

"I hope your elbow feels better!" Jonah says.

Huh? What is he talking about? What happened to her elbow?

Coco frowns. "How did you know I banged my elbow?"

"It was in your diary!" Jonah calls back.

Oh, no. Jonah did NOT just say that. Please tell me he didn't just say that.

He just said that.

"YOU READ MY DIARY?" she bellows. Her face is turning red.

I bang *my* elbow into Jonah's side. "Jonah!"

"What?" he says to me. "We're never going to see her again."

"HOW DARE YOU READ MY DIARY!" she yells. "I should throw you in prison!"

"We're sorry!" I yell up. "But you did leave it open on your desk," I add. "We didn't know it was your diary when we read it. And Jonah thinks you have very nice handwriting!"

"We'd better get out of here fast," Jonah says. "Ready?"

"Ready," I say.

He knocks once on the wall of the well. Twice. Three times.

We wait.

Nothing happens.

Ugh. "Maybe it's at the bottom of the well," I say.

"Huh?" Jonah asks.

"The bottom of the —" Never mind. "I'll do it."

I bend down and reach my hand all the way to the slimy bottom. Gross. I knock. Once. Twice. Three times.

Nothing.

"Now what?" I ask.

This time, Coco doesn't leave us in the well. Jonah climbs out on his own, but then both of them pull me up with the branch.

"I should have left you two after what you did," Coco says, when we're on dry land. "But I know my mom would want me to be nicer, so . . . how can I help?"

"I'm starving," Jonah says. He rubs his stomach.

Ruff. Prince is hungry, too.

"Come back to the palace," she says. "It's breakfast time. We're having omelets and hash browns."

"With ketchup?" Jonah asks.

"Of course," she says.

"We don't have time," I tell her, even though I'm so hungry I could eat three omelets. "It's six forty at home! We have to figure out what to knock on. Fast."

"I bet it's something at the castle. Let's go everyone!" Princess

Coco commands. With Coco in the lead, we all speed back to the palace.

"Can we look in your room?" I ask her, as I jump off Jonah's horse.

"All right," she says. But the minute we get there, she makes a big show of taking all her diaries and puts them in a wooden chest. She looks around her room. "I should probably put a lot of this stuff away, huh?"

"The toys do seem a little young for you," I say.

"Yeah. It's just . . . well, my mom bought this stuff for me. And I don't want to give anything away that came from her. I don't want to forget her."

I knew it! "You'll never forget her," I say, feeling sad for Coco but also understanding her better. "She's a part of you."

Coco nods. "She is. She even gave me my nickname. And you're right. It might be time to redecorate. Maybe Reginald's brother and sister want some of this stuff."

"I'm sure they do," I say. "That's really nice of you."

She grins. "I can be nice. Sometimes."

"Well, can you be nice now and help us look around?" I ask. "We need to find something, anything, that might be magical."

Jonah, Coco, and I each take a different section of the room. Even Prince sniffs around.

I try the mirror again just in case. But nope. It still doesn't work.

I see stuffed dragons. A desk and chair. A bureau. A wardrobe. A pink carpet. The chest containing her diaries.

"Are you sure there was nothing magical in the story of *The Frog Prince*?" Jonah asks me. He picks up the golden ball and knocks on it.

Nothing happens.

"Focus, Jonah, focus!" I shake my head. "Wait. There is one other thing."

"What?" he asks, catching the ball and holding on to it.

"Well, the wall," I remind him. "The princess throws the frog against the wall and —"

Wait. Why didn't I think of it before? Of course!

"The mural!" I cry. "Frederic thought I was his lucky charm because he changed back into a prince after *I* threw him against the wall, but it wasn't me. It was the mural."

"The mural!" Coco says, her eyes glistening. "My mother and I painted it together. I think this is one thing in my room I will keep the same."

Awww. I feel a little choked up.

We all approach the mural.

"Your mural is definitely magic," I tell Coco with a smile. "You don't mind if we knock on it, do you?"

"You threw a frog against it and the mural is fine," Coco says. "I think it can handle a knock."

Well, three knocks.

"Ready, Jonah?" I ask him.

"Ready!" Jonah says, scooping up Prince.

Except he still has the golden ball in his hand. "Give Coco back the ball," I tell him. "You can't take fairy tale stuff with you!"

Coco looks at the ball, then back at us. "He can keep it," she says.

Jonah's face lights up. "Thank you!" he says.

"Jonah —"

"She said I could!"

Sigh.

Coco holds up her hand. "On one condition," she adds. "As long as you promise never to read anyone's diary again."

"Promise," he says, flushing.

"Abby, you have to promise, too!" Coco says.

"Okay, I promise." I spot my flip-flops and put them back on.

"I guess this is good-bye, then," she says, and gives each of us a hug.

I hug her back. "Bye, Coco. Thank you for helping us."

"You'll be a super-cool commander in chief," Jonah tells her, smiling at his new ball.

"Time to go!" I say.

Ruff!

I knock once on the mural. Twice. Three times.

The braided rainbow on the wall starts to swirl.

"It's working!" Jonah calls.

"Good-bye, Coco!" I say.

Ruff!

We step through.

* Chapter Seventeen *

Home Again

We fall right onto the basement floor.

"We did it!" Jonah says. He tosses up the golden ball that Princess Coco gave him and lets Prince catch it.

We really did do it. I stand up and brush myself, facing the mirror.

Maybe now we can get some answers.

"Maryrose? Are you there?" I ask the mirror. "We want to talk to you! Jonah has your memories! And we stopped Prince Frederic from going back to Frogville! Is that what you wanted? Did we do the right thing?"

Jonah and I stare at the mirror. We can see our reflections. Prince sniffs the glass. Is something going to happen?

"Maryrose?" I call out again.

The mirror starts to ripple. Is that a face? It is! I see a face in the mirror! It's a woman with long wavy hair. She has a straight nose and a long chin. But it's a nice chin.

It's Maryrose! In the flesh. Well, not in the flesh. But in the mirror! I can see Maryrose! She exists!

"Hi," I say. "It's you!"

"Thank you," she says, "for saving Frederic's sister, Queen Sophie."

"You're welcome!" I say. "We would never have known Frederic was evil if it wasn't for Jonah's memories."

"I know," she says. "That's why he had them."

"I had them on purpose?" Jonah asks.

"Of course," Maryrose says.

"So you sent us on a mission?" I ask.

She nods. "I did."

"But, well, why didn't you just save her yourself?" I ask. "Why did you need us?"

"I would have if I could have," she says. "But the curse won't let me get back there."

"The curse?" I ask. "What curse?"

Her image starts to fade.

"Maryrose? Wait!"

She's gone. The mirror is still.

The ripples disappear.

"My head doesn't itch anymore," Jonah says after a minute. "I think the memories are gone."

I guess now that the job is done, the memories are done, too.

"I'm starving," Jonah says. "Do you think we could have omelets for breakfast?"

"Anything but frog legs." I look at my watch. Argh! "It's six fifty-five! Run! Run!"

We very quietly rush upstairs and into our rooms, Prince behind Jonah.

I toss off Princess Coco's wet clothes and change into fresh, dry pajamas. Ahhh.

Obviously, I forgot my other pair of pj's in Birdopolis.

Before I hop into my clean, dry bed, I take a peek at my magic jewelry box on my dresser. It shows me what all the fairy tale characters look like after I visit them.

Princess Coco's image on the box has changed. Instead of blowing a kiss to a frog, she's wearing the gold soldier's uniform while perched on her horse.

Perfect.

I pretend to be asleep and wait for my mom to come wake me up.

As soon as I get to school, I hear it.

"Crabby Abby!"

Right away I tense up. Brandon. Again. What is his problem? Why does he have to be so awful?

I can't help but wonder: Is it possible he's being mean because something is bothering him?

How can I tell if he's like Coco — a nice person who is being mean because he's upset — or if he's actually mean like Frederic?

How can anyone tell?

If only he had a diary . . .

I shake my head and laugh. No. I don't have to read his diary. I can do the next best thing.

I turn to look at him. "Hey, Brandon," I say. "How are you?"

He blinks. And then blinks again. "How am I?"

"Yes. How are you?"

He raises a thick eyebrow. "I'm fine," he spits out. He's very good at spitting.

"Is something the matter?" I ask.

He tilts his head. "What do you mean?"

"I don't know. I'm just wondering." I rack my brain to figure out how to ask. "What are you doing this weekend?"

He scowls. "Packing. I'm moving next month."

"You're moving?" I ask.

Brandon sticks his tongue out at the girl squeezing past us to get to her cubby. "Yes. Something wrong with your ears? I'm moving!" he whisper-yells.

I don't let him get to me. "Moving houses?"

His face kind of crumbles. "Yeah. And cities. I'm moving to Miami."

"You are?" I ask. "That's crazy! How come?"

"My mom got a new job," he mumbles. "She's going to be the Global Head of Content Partnerships for Mimford Media."

"I don't know what that means," I say.

"Me neither," he admits.

We're both quiet. Then I say, "It'll be really warm there."

He kicks his foot. "I guess."

Okay, now for the question that will tell me what I need to know. "Do you want to move?"

"I don't care," he mumbles. "Whatever."

He's lying. He totally does care. He's upset. That's why he's been so mean. He's like Coco! He's not really mean. He's just lashing out!

"This is great!" I exclaim.

His face darkens. "It's great that I'm moving? Thanks a lot."

"No, no, no. I didn't mean that. I mean . . . now I know why you've been acting the way you've been acting."

"How have I been acting?" he snaps.

"You've been . . . not so nice. But I have good news!"

He stares at me. "What's that?"

"It will be okay," I say.

"How do *you* know?"

"Because I moved, too!" I remind him. "At the beginning of the year. Remember?"

"Oh, yeah," he says. "I forgot." He looks down at me. "Was it hard?"

"Yeah," I admit. "At first. But you know what? Now I'm happy. Really happy. I have new friends. I've met all kinds of interesting people." I see Frankie, Robin, and Penny standing by the classroom door and looking at me like *Is she really talking to Brandon? And smiling?* "And I love my house," I add. I think of my room. And my basement. And my magic mirror. And all the adventures I never would have had if I hadn't moved from Naperville. "I'm glad I'm here."

He nods. "Thanks, Crabby Abby."

I laugh and shake my head. "Can you not call me that?"

He laughs, too. "What should I call you instead? Tabby Abby? Scabby Abby? Or just Abby?"

Hmm. "Fab Ab?" I suggest. "Or we can use alliteration. Awesome Abby? Amazing Abby? Those all work for me."

"You talk a lot. How about Gabby Abby?"

"I'll take it!"

I see that Frankie, Robin, and Penny are still watching me the end of the hall. They look very curious.

They wave me over.

"I gotta go, Brandon. No more fake-sneezing on Mad Libs, 'kay?"

He laughs. "Okay, Gabby Abby."

I walk over to Frankie, Robin, and Penny. They huddle around me.

"Was he bothering you?" Penny asks. "I tied my sneakers so tight this morning that even Brandon won't be able to step on the backs."

I don't think Brandon will be stepping on anyone's shoes. Or fake-sneezing on our Mad Libs. I think Brandon's mean days are over.

"Nope," I say. Frankie is on one side of me, and Robin on the other. Penny is next to Robin. I link my arms through Frankie and Robin's, and Penny links hers through Robin's. "Everything is just fine."

I look at my three friends — fine, two friends plus Penny — and know that everything is just great.

If it weren't for the fairy tales, I never would have understood why Brandon acted the way he did. Who knows what I'll discover next time? And maybe I'll learn more about who cursed Maryrose.

All I know for sure is that I can't wait to go back through my magic mirror.

Don't miss Abby and Jonah's next adventure,

where they fall into the tale of *Aladdin*!

Look for:

Whatever After #9: **GENIE IN A BOTTLE**

acknowledgments

Once upon a book, there was a very grateful author.

Thank you everyone at Scholastic, everyone at the Laura Dail Literary Agency, everyone at Deb Shapiro and Company, everyone at Lauren Walters and Co.: Aimee Friedman, Laura Dail, Tamar Rydzinski, Deb Shapiro, Lauren Walters, Katie Hartman, Jennifer Abbots, Abby McAden, David Levithan, Tracy van Straaten, Sheila Marie Everett, Caitlin Friedman, Bess Braswell, Whitney Steller, Jennifer Ung, Robin Hoffman, Sue Flynn, Terribeth Smith, Elizabeth Parisi, Emily Cullings, Lizette Serrano, and Emily Heddleson.

Thank you to all my friends, family, supporters, writing buddies, and first-readers. Targia Alphonse, Tara Altebrando, Bonnie Altro, Elissa Ambrose, Robert Ambrose, Jennifer Barnes, Emily Bender, the Bilermans, Jess Braun, Jeremy Cammy, Avery Carmichael, Ally Carter, the Dalven-Swidlers, the Finkelstein-Mitchells, Alan Gratz, the Greens, Adele Griffin, Anne Heltzel, Farrin Jacobs, Emily Jenkins, Maureen Johnson, Lauren Kisilevsky, Leslie Margolis, Maggie Marr, the Mittlemans, Aviva Mlynowski, Larry Mlynowski, Lauren Myracle, Jess Rothenberg, Melissa Senate, Courtney Sheinmel, Jennifer E. Smith, the Steins, Jill Swerdloff, the Swidlers,

Robin Wasserman, Louisa Weiss, the Wolfes, Maryrose Wood, Sara Zarr, and the downtown bus families.

Special shout-out to Chloe (who listened to the entire book and squealed at the right parts), Anabelle, and Todd: I love you. *Mwah!*

And of course, thank you, Whatever After readers. You are my princes and princesses.

Each time Abby and Jonah get sucked into their magic mirror, they wind up in a different fairy tale — and find new adventures!

Turn the page to read all about the *Whatever After* series!

Whatever After #1: FAIREST of ALL

In their first adventure, Abby and Jonah wind up in the story of Snow White. But when they stop Snow from eating the poisoned apple, they realize they've messed up the whole story! Can they fix it — and still find Snow her happy ending?

Whatever After #2: IF the SHOE FITS

This time, Abby and Jonah find themselves in Cinderella's story. When Cinderella breaks her foot, the glass slipper won't fit! With a little bit of magic, quick thinking, and luck, can Abby and her brother save the day?

Whatever After #3: SINK or SWIM

Abby and Jonah are pulled into the tale of the Little Mermaid — a story with an ending that is *not* happy. So Abby and Jonah mess it up on purpose! Can they convince the mermaid to keep her tail before it's too late?

Whatever After #4: DREAM ON

Now Abby and Jonah are lost in Sleeping Beauty's story, along with Abby's friend Robin. Before they know it, Sleeping Beauty is wide awake and Robin is fast asleep. How will Abby and Jonah make things right?

Whatever After #5: BAD HAIR DAY

When Abby and Jonah fall into Rapunzel's story, they mess everything up by giving Rapunzel a haircut! Can they untangle this fairy tale disaster in time?

Whatever After #6: COLD AS ICE

When their dog Prince runs through the mirror, Abby and Jonah have no choice but to follow him into the story of the Snow Queen! It's a winter wonderland . . . but The Snow Queen is rather mean, and she FREEZES Prince! Can Abby and Jonah save their dog . . . and themselves?

Whatever After #7: BEAUTY QUEEN

This time, Abby and Jonah fall into the story of *Beauty and the Beast.* When Jonah is the one taken prisoner instead of Beauty, Abby has to find a way to fix this fairy tale . . . before things get pretty ugly!

Don't miss this MAGICAL new series!

NORY, ELLIOTT, ANDRES, and BAX are students in Dunwiddle Magic School's UPSIDE-DOWN MAGIC class. In their classroom, lessons are unconventional, students are unpredictable, and magic has a tendency to turn wonky at the worst possible moments . . .

From *New York Times* bestselling authors SARAH MLYNOWSKI, LAUREN MYRACLE (*Life of Ty*), and EMILY JENKINS (*Toys Go Out*) comes a new, offbeat series about a group of misfits who set out to prove that life on the other side of ordinary has its charms.

about the author

Sarah Mlynowski is the author of the Magic in Manhattan series, *Gimme a Call*, and a bunch of other books for tweens and teens, including the Upside-Down Magic series, which she is cowriting with Lauren Myracle and Emily Jenkins. Originally from Montreal, Sarah now lives in the kingdom of Manhattan with her very own prince charming and their fairy tale–loving daughters. Visit Sarah online at www.sarahm.com and find her on Instagram, Facebook, and Twitter at @sarahmlynowski.